About the Author

Dawn Kulani loves to read when she isn't busy running around with her two teenage boys and husband, who lovingly call her a book addict. She enjoys camping and being with family and loves summertime when they can be outside enjoying the sunshine, which she says feeds her soul. Being of both Hawaiian and Scottish descent, she loves learning all about cultures, both her history and history in general. She has two crazy dogs, Silver and Nixie, and chickens who she enjoys watching play around.

How Not to Have a One Night Stand

Dawn Kulani

How Not to Have a One Night Stand

Chimera

CHIMERA PAPERBACK

© Copyright 2025
Dawn Kulani

The right of Dawn **Kulani**
to be identified as author of
this work has been asserted by her in accordance with the
Copyright, Designs and Patents Act 1988.

All Rights Reserved

No reproduction, copy or transmission of this publication
may be made without written permission.
No paragraph of this publication may be reproduced,
copied or transmitted save with the written permission or in accordance
with the provisions
of the Copyright Act 1956 (as amended).

Any person who commits any unauthorised act in relation to
this publication may be liable to criminal
prosecution and civil claims for damages.

A CIP catalogue record for this title is
available from the British Library.

ISBN 978-1-915451-10-1

This is a work of fiction. Names, characters, businesses, places, events
and incidents are either the products of the author's imagination or used
in a fictitious manner. Any resemblance to actual persons, living or
dead, or actual events is purely coincidental.

Trigger Warning – Violence, Age-Gap Bondage, Death, Mention of
drugs, Parental abandonment, Cheating (not between MC) , Betrayal,
Pregnancy

Chimera is an imprint of
Pegasus Elliot MacKenzie Publishers Ltd.
www.pegasuspublishers.com

First Published in 2025

**Sheraton House Castle Park
Cambridge England**
Printed & Bound in Great Britain

Dedication

To my boys, never give up on your dreams, and always know how much I love you.

Acknowledgments

I have been working on this for a long time and can't believe it's finally a book. This has been a dream come true. First and foremost, thank you to the readers. I appreciate you giving my story a chance. I want to give a big shout-out to my husband. Without your support and encouragement, I don't know if this would've been possible. Thank you for being my sounding board; your thoughts and ideas on getting some of these scenes right made all the difference. This also couldn't have been done without my sister; she is my biggest cheerleader and genuinely the best person I know in this world. Thank you for being you! I can't go without giving a special thank you to my Aunt Cathy. Your love and support made me know I could do this. I hope you know how much your support means to me. Last but not least, thank you to the team of people who helped turn this from just words I wrote on paper into a beautiful book. Anyone who has ever thought you weren't enough or couldn't do something, just know that you are not alone and that you are strong. You can do this; never give up. With love, Dawn Kulani…

Emmy

There were a lot of ways I had pictured celebrating my twenty-first birthday. Sitting at the corner of this dimly lit grunge bar alone was not one of them.

I swirled the amber-colored liquid around the glass of Brandy I had been nursing for the past couple hours, watching it pass over the bar's logo for the millionth time. I was far from "Tipsy," as the logo suggested.

The latest song playing on the jukebox mixed with the rising voices of the people trying to talk over each other.

Tipsy Roots Bar and Grill wasn't a bar designed for the younger crowd, nothing hip or trendy about it. It had a couple booths, a few tables, a jukebox, dart board, and some pool tables. It smelled like old wood and grease; it wasn't fancy by any means.

That's one of the things that drew me here, I didn't want to go to a bar that felt like a frat party. I wanted a fun night out with my best friend. So, when Lucy had originally suggested we come here for my birthday, I was excited.

Checking my phone again, knowing Lucy still wouldn't have answered back, I hadn't heard anything from her since she said she was going to her parents earlier today.

She is going to have some explaining to do when I finally get a hold of her. I know her parents are strict on no phones when they are all together and all, but today wasn't just any ordinary day; it was supposed to be our day out.

And right about now, I was second-guessing my decision to still come here, knowing full well I would be alone.

What a way to celebrate my twenty-first birthday, my golden birthday, Aug 21! This was supposed to be the best birthday of my life, right? That's what all tradition says anyway: your magical birthday when the day matches the year you're turning. Well, so far, it has been the same as any other birthday—me alone, being mostly forgotten.

Sighing, I shotgun the rest of the drink. Wincing a little, as the fire from the liquor burned down my throat.

Victory! I had officially finished off my first drink since legally being able to buy alcohol.

I set the empty glass on the bartop with a clink, giving the intimidating bartender a smile.

Trying not to let him get under my skin. The mysterious bartender I'll refer to as Mr. Tattoo, since he's not wearing a name tag, is a large, muscled man with tattooed arms and dark hair who has said very little to me all night. He's just watched me as I sit here alone for hours, which has only added to the intimidation and embarrassment.

Taking another look around the bar, I scan the other patrons, noticing—not for the first time tonight—a man at the other end of the bar looking me over intently.

I didn't know what his problem is, but I'm currently in no mood to deal with another asshole tonight.

I had already had to tell off a few guys earlier; I think it had amused Mr. Tattoo, as that was about the only time he showed any other expression besides stone cold.

Why every guy in here thinks that a girl in a bar alone is just waiting for them is beyond me.

Just because I'm here alone does not mean it's an open invitation to hit on me.

I was having such a shit afternoon since my best friend stood me up, and to top it off, my mom decided tomorrow was a great day for her to get married for the third time.

This is supposed to be my big weekend, and I don't even care how selfish I sound right now. Every once in a while, being a little selfish is needed.

I had spent so much of my time pushing to be the best, to finish school top of my class, to make everyone proud, to make sure I wasn't a disappointment that I just felt why couldn't I have this one weekend for me.

It's not that I don't like my soon-to-be stepdad, he's definitely better than the ones before him. It's just that this will be her third husband, and she could have planned it at another time, like any weekend besides this one.

Part of me still feels a little guilty about thinking like this, though, because she stuck with her first two husbands a lot longer than she should have with the thought that she was doing what I needed. She had tried to make her relationships work so that I had a "normal" family, whatever that looks like.

Her problem was she chose shit guys who didn't really want the insta family.

My mom is a beautiful woman. The crap men she chose wanted her badly enough to put up with the baggage she came with, me, for a little while anyway.

At least, I wasn't a little kid anymore, so this one doesn't have to play Daddy Dearest or pretend to want to be in my life—not that he seems like that type. No, this one is far different from the past guys, and for that I am grateful.

Shaking myself from my thoughts, I decide it's about time for me to leave. As my luck would have it, the creepy guy that has been staring me down is now heading my way.

"Hey there, beautiful, I couldn't help but notice you were here alone." He turns to the bartender and says, "Another drink for the pretty lady."

Mr. Tattoo quickly pours me another Brandy, sitting it in front of me.

"No thanks," I reply, pushing the freshly poured glass back toward Mr. Tattoo. He doesn't take the drink back or say anything; he just stands there watching our interaction with his arms folded across his chest.

I want to roll my eyes at him. "Gee, thanks, man."

"Excuse me!" Mr. Creepy says with annoyance.

"I'm not interested, thanks," I answer back in my forced, cheery tone.

Pushing the chair back, I go to stand up. Just as the creep man grabs hold of my upper arm, gripping it tightly.

As he does, I notice the bartender straighten, unfolding his arms and taking a step forward.

"I offered you a drink; you don't need to be a bitch about it; just sit back down and enjoy the free drink, darling."

Yanking my arm free, I grab the drink that was still sitting on the bartop and dump it on the man.

His hands flail in the air, cursing as he tries to get the liquid off him.

Watching him nearly makes me burst out in laughter.

"You're right, I definitely enjoyed that drink," I say with a smile.

I hear the bartender trying to stifle a laugh. I glance over at him, and he's got a smirk on his face; it looks almost out of place for the big man.

I turn, walking away without another glance at the creep, who is now furious and shouting profanities at me.

Thank God, he doesn't come after me as I keep walking away.

Not really paying attention to where I'm going, I turn down the small hallway toward the ladies room, running straight into a solid wall of a person.

"Oh shit, sorry."

Stepping back, slightly, I look up at the man I would have plowed over had he not been built like a brick wall. His dark hair, just long enough to style, shorter on the sides with longer waves on top, has the faintest dusting of gray coming in on the sides near his temples, and his well-trimmed beard is lightly salted as well.

I look him up and down, taking in all of the man in front of me—the way his black collared button-up shirt hugs his muscled form, the sleeves rolled up just below his elbows, and the way the dark blue jeans he's wearing fit, oh, so perfect on him.

He could be a god damn model, I think to myself, swallowing as my mouth waters.

"Like what you see?" He smirks, raising one eyebrow.

I can feel the blush as it begins to spread pink across my cheeks.

Realizing I had been openly ogling the poor man.

"I do," I blurt out

He lets out a small laugh. "Good."

Oh, shit. I did not mean to say that out loud. I usually don't have that amount of confidence. His rough voice sends shivers through my body.

"If you could excuse me, I need to pee," I finally say after continuing to stare at him for far longer than polite.

"By all means." He steps back and motions down the hallway.

What the hell was I thinking? I am never that forward, and he has to be close to twice my age.

Once safely in the stall, I quickly do my business. As I am pulling up my bottoms, I hear the bathroom door creak open, followed by a clicking sound that sounds offly like the lock being put in place.

"*Um*, someone is in here," I yell through the stall. I flush and head out when there is no reply.

Walking out of the stall, I am completely stunned to see the man from the hall leaning against the sink counter.

"What do you think you're doing?"

"Just admiring the view," he says smugly.

Great, a sexy hunk with a complex.

I make my way to the sink next to where he is standing, wash up, and turn to walk toward the door, determined to just ignore him.

I have had enough overbearing men for one evening.

"I have a proposition for you," he says, stopping me in my tracks.

"Oh, is that so?" Amusement evident in my tone.

He shifts, pushing himself off the sink, standing, he walks until he's right in front of me. Filling in the already small space. I try to take a step backward, and meet with the wooden door that touches my back.

"Yeah, it's so."

The weird heat I feel next to him makes me blush, and his rough voice sending those shivers through me again, which I've only read about in books. Tilting my head to the side, I look away.

He grabs my face gently with one hand and lifts my chin, so that I am looking into his hazel eyes.

"I don't know why, but you intrigue me, Angel. And I would very much like to spend a night with you."

I scuff. "Really, now that's forward."

But damn if the heat now coursing through me didn't want to make me say, "Okay, sure, let's go." I inhale deeply, wishing I could back up more, put some space between us.

"I'm not one to beat around the bush, and I am not asking for anything crazy, just one night."

"So, you're trying to take advantage of a young drunk girl in a bar? Is this your usual pick-up? Are you some kind of creeper?"

I try to hide how much he's actually affecting me. Squeezing my thighs together as the heat pools between my legs.

He laughs lightly. The sound sends goosebumps down my arms.

"No, No. I don't make a habit of picking up people from the bar. I also know from watching you tonight that you have only had one drink in the four hours you've been here, so you are far from drunk, Angel. If you don't want to take me up on my offer, that's fine. You just seemed like someone who could use a good time."

He reaches past me, unlocking the door, stepping sideways. I step forward out of the way as he walks out the door.

Just like that, he was gone.

What was with this guy?

Better yet, why am I questioning going after him?

I splash some cool water on my face before heading out.

I think I'm just over tonight; it has been weird and not at all the fun time I was hoping to have tonight.

The guy was right, though. I could use a little release. It has been almost a year since I'd had sex, and just the guy's voice had the moisture building down there.

I take a quick look around the bar, searching for him, but he's nowhere in sight.

Guess I missed that opportunity. I shrug to myself.

I close out my tab, toss a little tip to Mr. Tattoos, and walk out of the bar.

Now that I'm walking alone to my car, I wish even more that I would have taken him up on his offer; it seems a hell of a lot better than sitting alone the rest of the night wallowing in my own self-pity. Besides, isn't that what your twenties are for—experiences and mistakes?

The gravel parking lot wasn't large, but I had parked on the end away from the door, another decision I was now regretting. The orange glow of the lot lights barely illuminated the place.

I couldn't help but think they should really invest in better lighting. I'm less than three feet from my car when a hand comes out from nowhere, grabbing my arm. Spinning around, I try to get out of their grasp. But I can't; I'm now face-to-face with a very pissed off man.

Great, the creepy asshole from earlier. I can smell the Brandy on him from the drink I spilt. He shoves me backward hard enough that I stumble, and my back hits my car.

"Didn't you get the message the first time, asshole?" I spit out.

"You need to learn some manners, you little bitch."

I slide down my car in an attempt to crawl past, as he gets closer. The gravel below me crunches, and my attempt to crawl away is halted by the yanking of my hair. A firm grip pulls me back to my feet.

I kick backward, trying to hit any part of him, but he's too close.

He's standing so close that I can feel the grease from his hair rubbing along my cheek, and the strong smell of the alcohol—it's more than just the Brandy coming off him; he smells like he drank half the bar.

He slams me back down, and my head hits the hard metal hood of my car, connecting with a thud.

Well, shit, that hurts and is going to leave a bruise. I can't help but think about how my mom is going to be pissed if I ruin her wedding photos.

Dizziness sets in almost immediately.

He holds me down, smashing my face into the hood, the weight of his body pressing hard against me. He's basically on top of me, gripping my hair tightly in his fist.

Wiggling I tried to get out from under him, but that was just making him happy.

"Yeah, darling, grind that ass into me." The unmistakable poke of his erection pressing against my back.

I want to throw up. "Fuck you." I grit out, trying to think of a way to get out of his grip.

Suddenly, I'm yanked backward again. I brace myself, waiting for the next blow. It doesn't come; instead, I free fall to the ground. Palms flat, I push against the gravel, barely stopping myself from a full-face plant. I shuffle, flipping over into a sitting position.

Blinking to adjust my eyes, my vision a little blurred from getting hit on my head and the ever-darkening sky. They really should require better lights in parking lots.

Someone else has the creepy asshole pinned to the ground.

"I think the lady asked you to leave her alone," a deep voice booms, laced in anger.

"I should kill you for laying hands on her," he says through a clenched jaw as his fists connect solidly to the creeper's face.

The sound of a bone crunching fills the air, and I can see the splatter of blood even in the poor lighting.

I gasp, covering my mouth with my hands.

I don't even know the man, but I can tell he's not making an idle threat. I'm pretty sure he's about to beat this man to death with his bare hands.

My gasp stops the man mid-swing, halting his fist from landing another blow as he turns in my direction. He looks at me like he has forgotten I was even there. He climbs off the guy he just about beat to death, turning to land a heavy kick to his side before stepping away, heading in my direction.

I'm not sure how the man on the ground has the strength to get up, but he does, grunting with each movement.

Watching in shock as the man who just attacked me pushes off the ground, stumbling to his feet, blood running down his swollen face. A fresh, pungent smell drifts in the air, making it apparent that he peed himself.

Wasting no time, he turns running off in the opposite direction.

I sit motionless, I can't believe what just happened.

The man from the bathroom walks calmly over to me. All I can think is, damn, he looks good, all alpha male energy, even with the blood splatter covering his hands and face.

"Are you okay?" he asks. Wiping his hands on his pants before bending down, reaching out offering his hand to me.

Without hesitation, I take the outstretched hand. He firmly but gently pulls me to my feet.

I feel like I'm on display as he looks me over. With the hand not currently still holding mine, he runs his knuckles lightly across my cheek. I wince, even though his touch is soft. I can feel my cheek is already starting to swell.

"I'm fine," I say nervously.

"You don't look fine," he snaps.

"What a lovely thing to say to a lady."

He looks down at me, still brooding. Walking me a few feet backward, he releases my hand from his, and using both hands, he grabs me by the waist, picking me up like I weigh nothing, sitting me on the hood.

"Let me clean you up a bit."

"I'm fine. Besides, you look like you need to clean up more than I do."

He ignores me and pulls a handkerchief from his pocket. Who carries a handkerchief anymore?

Without further discussion, he begins to dab at a small cut on my forehead—one I didn't even know was there. Great another thing for my mom to bitch about.

I don't know if it's from his close proximity, hitting my head, or both, but I am feeling light-headed. He smells as sexy as he looks. Like fresh air and lemon but with a hint of something else, either from his soap or an expensive cologne.

"Pretty great way to spend your birthday, *huh*?"

"Well, I could think of better ways," he says in a deep, low voice.

"Oh, God, is he still flirting with me?"

"Have you always been this egotistical?"

"Not at all, like I said earlier, I just don't shy away from what I want. I find no use in playing those kinds of games."

I can't help but ask, "What kind of games do you like to play?"

"Ones that would have you running far away, Angel."

His tone turns sensual, it has me thinking about all things erotic and sends heat in all the right places.

"Try me."

There I go again, saying what I'm thinking, not what I should be saying. Especially after just watching him almost kill someone.

A wicked grin crossed his face.

"Have you been rethinking my offer?"

"That's not what I meant," I stutter.

"Whatever you say, Angel."

It should annoy me that he keeps calling me that, but something in the way he says it makes me tingle.

He steps back, giving me another once-over.

I look down; my white shirt is covered in dirt and my blue jeans too.

"Best I can do out here."

"Thanks, doc. I think I'll make it."

"It's Adrian."

"What's Adrian?"

"My name."

"Oh, I'm Emmy. Nice to meet you, Adrian." I blink up at him dumbly; of course, he was telling me his name.

I don't know that I have even taken in all that has just happened yet; my head feels a bit heavy and still being next to him makes me feel on edge in a different way.

"Nice to meet you, Emmy, although not exactly how I pictured this happening."

Before I say more that I shouldn't be saying, like, oh, how did you see it happening? I slide down the hood of my car, trying to stand.

"I better get going," I say, wobbling from the slight dizziness.

Adrian's arms wrap around my waist, steadying me.

"Whoa there." I don't think you should be driving.

"It's just a little light headedness from, I don't know... maybe hitting my head on my car. I'll wait a few minutes to let it pass, then I'll be fine."

"Are you always this stubborn?"

"No, it seems to be a new trait, just for you," I say sarcastically.

He lets me go, crossing his arms against his chest.

I instantly miss the heat his touch burns into me with each contact.

There is no denying that I am sexually attracted to this man, and I bet whatever he had in mind for tonight would be something that would have been amazingly fun.

Most definitely better than getting the shit kicked out of me in a parking lot.

"Fine, Adrian, I will let you take me home. But I really can't leave my car here; I have to be somewhere pretty early tomorrow."

"Not a problem, Angel; I will have someone follow us in it."

He pulls out his phone, typing away.

"He will be out in a minute."

A minute later, Mr. Tattoos, the bartender, walks out of the bar holding something in his hand. He walks over and hands me the bag he was holding, seeing it's an ice pack.

"Thanks."

Adrian grabs the keys from me and hands them over to him.

"Come, I'll take you in my car."

My mind immediately went dirty at those words, more proof I should have taken him up on his offer for a one-nighter. I apparently need to get laid.

Following him a few stalls over, Adrian steps to the passenger side of a sleek black Cresting 7 series, opening the door for me to climb in. I have seen enough true crime to know that I should most definitely be questioning my judgment right now. I do, however, have the right frame of mind to send a text off to Lucy just in case.

Me: Met a HOT man at the bar; he drives a black Cresting 7; if I don't show up tomorrow, send Lifetime my story.

"Wowwee, fancy." I whistle out as I sit in the soft leather seats. Sure beats the hell out of my second hand junker.

"It's just a car." He grunts.

"If you say so."

Adrian leans over to the passenger side, and for a minute, I think he's going to kiss me. Instead, he reaches into the glove box, pulling out some wet wipes. My heart races, and I internally kick myself.

"Where to, Angel?" he asks after wiping the majority of the blood from his hands and face.

I roll my eyes at him. "Why do you keep calling me that?"

He pauses, seeming to think about his answer.

"I watched you walk into the bar, and the first thing that came to my mind was, look at that angel, with your golden hair perfectly cascading in waves down your shoulders, your honey brown eyes so big and bright, and those pink lips..." he trails off.

"*Hmm*, I didn't even notice you before I ran into you."

"No, you wouldn't have; I was in the back hallway. But trust me, I saw you right away, lighting up the whole room, hips swaying in those jeans that look painted on."

"You sure you aren't a creepy perv that just waits in bars? Cuz it sure sounds like it."

He lets out a deep guttural laugh.

"I own Tipsy Roots. I saw you on the security camera in the office."

"Oh."

Well, hell, this man owns a bar, while I am out here avoiding making any life decisions for myself.

"So where to?" he asks again, pulling out of the parking lot.

I don't know what comes over me—the no filter thing again.

"Your place."

I sit back and put the ice pack on my cheek, thinking I must be losing my damn mind.

I'm in a car with a stranger who literally just beat the piss out of someone, then doesn't say another word about it acting like it didn't even happen. Even though he had to wipe blood off himself, his clothes are still covered in it.

Yet somehow, in this very moment, I am fine with all of it.

Adrian

I almost lose focus on the road when I hear those words come out of her mouth.

"Your place."

I hold in a groan. Damn, my little Angel is just as forward as she keeps claiming me to be.

I'll have to thank my brother later for being stupid enough to be marrying someone he barely knows, or I wouldn't even be in town to meet this gorgeous golden-haired beauty in my passenger seat.

I should feel bad; she's young. But I have needed to be near her since I saw her on the monitor, walking in my bar. Her perfect hips swaying in those ass hugging jeans, the faintest peeking of cleavage in that tight tank, and those fucking lips. Lips so perfect, I've wanted to taste all night.

I stir slightly in my seat to hide the fact that my cock is now stiffening against my jeans.

"What?" I ask just to make sure I heard her right.

"I said your place." She pauses before adding, "Unless you've changed your mind."

"Just making sure you know what you're saying."

"I didn't hit my head that hard. I'm fully capable of making decisions, I promise."

I glance over at her; she's got her head pressed to the back of the seat and the ice pack on her cheek. The small cut I wiped earlier doesn't seem like it will leave a mark. But her face will be purple tomorrow.

The thought of that guy's hands on her makes my blood boil. Had she not been there staring up at me, he'd be a dead man right now. I have never wanted to hurt someone so badly as I did the second I saw him on top of her. The rage was instant; I have never killed a man but, in that moment, I knew I could and would have, and he dared lay a hand on my angel. Had she not gasped, pulling me from the rage.

I shake my head slightly. What am I even thinking. She's not mine. The reaction wasn't just because it was her; I would have felt that same level of rage no matter what girl that asshole had attacked.

Which is partly true; I would have beat the shit out of any man who dared lay a hand on any female. But I'm not going to lie to myself and act like the possessiveness over her isn't more, and the sexual tension between us has me on edge.

I haven't felt like this in a long time. I can't even remember if I have ever truly felt this level of instant possessiveness. I need to remind myself that I don't have feelings; I don't do anything that I don't control, at least not anymore.

She's like a forbidden fruit; come to tempt me. Now that I think about it, I better make sure she isn't actually forbidden. It wouldn't be the first time an underage girl used a fake ID to get into one of my bars.

I don't mind her being younger, but I mind very much if she is underage.

Emmy sighs, her breathing getting lighter, her chest falling in soft rhythm. The adrenalin must be wearing off, but I can't let her sleep either, not until I can give her a good look over in real lighting to make sure she doesn't have a concussion.

She might need medical attention. I'll handle that, if needed.

"Emmy." I try to speak as softly as possible.

When she doesn't reply, I reach over and touch her thigh, giving it a little squeeze.

"Emmy," I repeat softly.

Her eyes flutter open with those big, beautiful eyes. "Oh sorry."

"We are almost there; you just can't go to sleep yet, Angel."

"Oh, your plans include letting me sleep tonight?" She smiles.

Fuck me, she is going to be a hand full. It makes my cock jerk in my pants. I feel like a damned teenager.

A short drive later, and we are pulling into my driveway.

"You live in Entrada?" she says squinting out of the tinted windows of the car.

"I do, part of the time. I have another place just outside of Portland, Oregon, where I usually spend my time. I have a bar there as well."

"Fancy."

I step out and around the car to open the door for her, helping her out.

The driveway and path lighting cast just enough glow to see her clearly taking in the house. It's smaller for this area, with only four bedrooms but has a great view of the lake and golf course. The exterior is light red stucco and blends into the surrounding area. The red rock landscape is one of the best things about southern Utah.

I walk her in through the large, rustic wooden door at the main entrance. I enjoy seeing her face light up with every detail she takes in; it's like seeing the place for the first time again, making me not even remember all the reasons she shouldn't be here with me.

We walk through the door and are greeted with the large gray columns that frame the entryway that lead into the open kitchen. The same stone also adorns the stove area, surrounded by light wood cabinets. Across from the island is the living room with a fireplace that matches the rest of the stone and wooden mantel.

"Your place is beautiful."

"Thank you," I say, trying not to think of how empty this place usually feels to me.

Taking her hand, I walk her into the kitchen. "Let me look at your bruises; come here." I pick her up, placing her on the granite island countertop.

She makes the most adorable squeal.

"Already showing bruising. The ice has seemed to help the swelling a little."

"See, Doc, just fine."

"Does it hurt anywhere else?"

"Nope. My poor face got the worst of it."

"I shouldn't have let him walk away so easily," I say as I turn her hands over in mine and see the scratches marring her palms from the gravel.

She lifts her hands from mine, placing one hand on my forearm and one on my jaw, rubbing against my beard.

"I'm fine. Because of you. I think you did enough. You brutally maimed someone for me, and I haven't even said thank you."

"You don't owe me a thank you."

I can't help it. I move my hand to cover the one on my jawline. I selfishly want her to keep touching me.

"I do; it could have been way worse. I don't know what he was planning on doing to me. So, thank you."

She leans up from the counter, by large frame preventing her from slipping over the edge. She plants a soft kiss on to my lips. Shocking the hell out of me.

Emmy's honey-colored eyes go bright as she sits back, dropping her hands to her side. A look of shock briefly crosses her own face, like she wasn't expecting herself to do that either. Just as quickly, she hides it behind a smile.

"You're welcome, Angel."

"Now that I am sure you aren't going to pass out on me, and I don't think you need medical attention, even though I do think you might have a mild concussion, what made you say you would come to my place?"

I help her off the counter, purely out of need to feel that connection I get everytime I touch her and the little shiver her body makes as I wrap my arms around her.

"I don't know." She shrugs. "I almost followed you out of the bathroom, to be honest."

"Did you now?" I give her that same devilish smirk and raised eyebrow.

Her breath catches; she's so close to me that her body is pressing into mine. I love the curves of her body. She's not some starving cheerleader type; she is lean but has beautiful curves too; her breasts aren't small but they aren't large. They look like they would fit perfectly in my hands, and I can't wait to grab around those hips and ass; her thighs aren't sticks either. They have a little meat to them, and I love it. Makes me feel like I could be as rough as I want with her, and it won't break her.

I am a good foot taller than her, and I love how she has to look up at me.

I lean down and kiss along her exposed neck. Emmy's breathing becomes faster. I love every tiny sound she makes.

I stop myself from going further. Straightening and stepping back from her.

The parts of her cheeks that aren't sporting the bruise are a pretty rose pink for me, a sign that hopefully means I have the same effect on her as she does on me.

"I want to make sure we are on the same page before this goes any further."

Emmy nods. "Okay," she says breathily.

"First off, how old are you, Emmy?"

"Twenty-one today. So, yes, I am a consenting adult and have been for three years."

Shit, she is young.

"Well, you might change your mind. I'm thirty-eight."

"So. That doesn't change that I am attracted to you; besides, this is just a night of fun, right?"

"Just making sure, you really want to do this."

"You aren't married, have any diseases, a murderer, or into causing bodily harm, right?"

I have been known to like a little pain in the bedroom, but I would never leave a permanent mark. I like a little bondage and whips from time to time.

"Not married, regularly tested, clean, not a murderer, and no bodily harm, but I would love to show you how pleasurable adding a little pain can be if you're willing."

She rubs her hand, thumb, and pointer finger across her chin. "Maybe something I would consider."

"Well, in that case, then I think we are on the same page."

"The night is still young," she says.

On that, I grab her back up into my arms and carry her to my bedroom. I plop her down, and she giggles as she hits the plush mattress.

"If at any time you change your mind, all you need to do is tell me to stop."

"Got it. Now kiss me."

"*Mmm,* so demanding, my little Angel."

"Who am I to deny her?"

Climbing onto the bed spreading her legs as I crawl between them, placing my arms on both sides of her to hold my large frame above her. I bend my elbows and lower just enough to reach her lips.

She places one hand on my chest caressing through my shirt. I pull back, remembering the shirt is still covered in dried blood splatter.

She looks up at me, confused. "Did I do something wrong?"

"No, Angel, I just need to clean up real quick first."

I lean down and kiss her hard, crushing my mouth to hers in a quick claim.

"I'll be right back."

I make a quick exit to the ensuite, stripping my bloody clothes and tossing them in the laundry bin.

I don't want to leave her for long. I turn on the water, not waiting for it to get warm and quickly wash.

Grabbing a nearby towel off the rack, I dry off, grabbing my sweatpants from the attached closet before walking back into the room.

Emmy is still lying where I left her just minutes ago, fully clothed with her head resting on the pillow, she has clearly fallen asleep.

Looking even more like an angel than before, with her golden hair sprawled around her like a halo.

I am half-tempted to just tuck her in and climb in next to her. But that would be something someone who cares would do, and my selfishness takes over as all I can think about is tasting her, something I have imagined doing all night.

I lean down, kissing her cheek and whispering into her ear.

"You're so fucking beautiful."

Emmy's eyes pop open. "Did I fall asleep?"

"It's okay, Angel," I say and climb back on the bed next to her.

She smiles and moves, so she is now straddling me, leaning down, and nipping at my lip before she works her tongue into my mouth, almost frenzied. She rubs down my chest, and I love the feel of her hands on my bare skin.

Quickly stripping off her shirt, I'm pleased to find her perfect breast in just a lace bra. I cup them, squeezing softly, pinching her nipples between the lacy fabric.

I knew they would fit perfectly in my palms.

I release her breasts and caress down her back and sides, coming around to undo the front of her jeans.

She laughs, breaking away from our kiss. "Can't really get undressed this way."

"I guess not."

I grab her waist as she goes to dismount me, flipping her onto her back.

"Stay still," I tell her as I begin trailing kisses down her body, starting along her neck, painfully slowly working my way down until I reach the fabric just below her belly button. I finish undoing her jeans and slide them down and off her legs. To my enjoyment, she is wearing matching lace panties, that don't leave much to the imagination. Restarting my exploration of her perfect body, I kiss her ankles, caressing my way back up her legs, alternating sides.

"Spread wider."

Emmy obeys immediately, granting me further access to her. Such a good girl. I take her legs and place them over my shoulders. I can smell her arousal, burying my face into her pussy I tease through the fabric with my tongue before moving her panties to the side, so that I can slip a finger into her; she is wet and warm. Pumping in and out of her slowly, I add a second finger, and she clenches around them.

Taking my time working my fingers in and out of her while I lick and suck that perfect little clit, her moans and gasps fuel me on. I look up at her chest, heaving up and down as she tries to control her breathing while I take her closer to orgasm. She grips the sheets to help steady her. Her hips buck.

"Don't stop. Please don't stop." She pants as I slip my fingers out of her.

"Wouldn't dream of it, Angel."

Sliding her panties off and tossing them to the floor with her other discarded clothes.

"Now I'm going to make you cum on my tongue."

I lick her slit, slipping my tongue inside, lapping her juices like a starving kitten. Grabbing her ass and pulling her up into me so that I can get deeper, she tastes like honey on my tongue, sweeter than I could have imagined, and I can't get enough.

I am quickly rewarded as she goes over the edge. Her body is shaking beneath my touch.

Emmy

I didn't even know it could feel that good with just a tongue, not to mention the extra tickle of his beard between my thighs.

Still reeling from the orgasm, Adrian gently places my legs back on the bed. I try to slow my breathing; it's impossible with the look he's giving me, licking his lips like he's just tasted the best thing in the world. It has me wanting more, and my body reacts immediately.

Adrian strips off his sweats, and for the first time I get the full view of his amazing body. He may be seventeen years older than me, but he has not let his body go. The man must hit the gym frequently; he should be a cover model for romance novels. I know I'd buy it just to keep looking at him. His light pattering of chest hair is short, well kept, and sports the same faint signs of graying amongst the dark hair, just like his beard.

I want to rub my fingers through it.

"Now that you're all warmed up, ready for some fun?"

"Yes, please."

Sitting up, I unclip my bra, the last remaining item keeping me from being totally naked.

Adrian walks back toward me, leaning over, wrapping a hand around the back of my neck, and scooting me to the edge of the bed. He leans down, kissing me hard with such passion. I can taste myself on him as he slips his tongue between my parted lips, mingling with mine. His other hand finds my nipple, taking it between his fingers, he rubs each in turn into firm points, adding a little extra pressure as I weave my fingers through his hair.

"I have a little present for these," he says, breaking the kiss.

I don't even recognize the little whimper that escapes my mouth as he pulls away. This man has me so intoxicated. "Do you want the present, Angel?"

"Yes."

"Good girl."

I watch as Adrian walks to a small end table on the side of the bed, opening a drawer. He pulls out a couple things, but I can't quite see from this angle and his body blocking most of the view.

He comes back holding what looks like chain, I can't fathom what the heck he's going to do with such a small piece of chain. Then I notice the ends of the chain have little clamps on them.

Swallowing, I take a deep breath. I have never done anything like this. What was I thinking when I was being so forward and carefree earlier?

My body shivers with a mix of nervousness and excitement.

Adrian must notice my body tense.

"You can say no; I will stop."

"I don't know if I want you to stop or not," I answer honestly.

"I did say I was open to trying things."

"Here, let me see your finger."

I hold my hand out to him, and he gently takes it, turning it palm up. He shows me the clamp; it's a metal chain with alligator clamps on each end, and the clamps have a black rubber coating on the tips. Adrian takes one of the clamps and clips it to the tip of my pinky. Using the little twist thing, he tightens it down a bit. It grips it tightly, adding a small amount of pressure; it doesn't hurt, but that's on my pinky, not my nipple.

"I promise, I won't do anything to harm you," he says and unclamps it.

"Okay, I'll try it."

"Up on your knees for me, Angel."

I do as he asks and switch so that I'm kneeling on the bed, this gives him access to me without having to bend down.

He tosses the other thing he grabbed onto the bed next to me, and looking down, I notice it's just a condom. Oh, good, not another device. I breathe heavily.

Taking my breast into his mouth, he sucks and nips at my nipples, peaking them back up until they are hard points. My eyes close, and my head tilts backward.

Adrian effectively took any other thoughts out of my mind. The only thing I can think about now is the need and want to let him do whatever he wants to me, because so far it has all been amazing.

I draw in a deep breath as the first clamp is put into place; the pressure way more intense than it was on my finger. I welcome the pain as the wetness builds between my legs again.

I almost lose it completely when he clasps the second one on and gives them a little tug.

He was not kidding earlier when he said pain for pleasure. The arousal surprises me.

Now this is a way to celebrate your birthday. Had I known how amazing it could be, I would have tried to have a one-night stand before.

"Open your eyes."

Taking in another steading breath and slowly letting it out, I look up and meet his beautiful hazel eyes. They are smoldering with desire.

No one has ever looked at me like that, ever.

"I want you to ride me now, Angel."

I don't say anything, just nod. He climbs onto the bed, lying down in the center. My gaze goes down to his very hard cock, which currently has his hand wrapped around it, stoking it. I didn't know watching someone could be such a turn-on. He reaches for me, guiding me over to him. I throw one leg over his body to straddle him. He grabs the condom off the bed, ripping the packet, he hands it to me.

Slipping it on, I can feel his pulse as he reacts to my touch. It gives me a boost of confidence. I rub up and down with my hand a couple times, mimicking his earlier movements. Once I can't take the wait any longer, I position myself to take him in. Gripping my waist, he guides me down onto his shaft, sliding down slowly until he fills me completely.

I slowly begin to rock up and down, and the metal chain slaps against my stomach as I ride him. The little clamps pull gently on my nipples with each pump. I press my palms flat on his chest as he thrusts up under me, meeting me in each movement.

We are slow at first, but as he guides me, getting faster and deeper. When we are at a good pace, Adrian surprises me, releasing his grip on my waist. He reaches up with one hand and grabs hold of the chain, giving it a little tug. It's a shot of pain that makes me scream out; the sensation is quickly replaced by the pleasure that spreads through my whole body.

Panting and out of breath, I feel the wave of ecstasy getting closer; I know Adrian is close too, his breathing heavier and his movements harder.

All of a sudden, I am flipped on my back, and he slides almost all the way out of me.

I moan in protest.

He removes the nipple clamp, and the unexpected release of pressure is just as intoxicating as the pain was.

"Good girl," he says and sheaths himself into me fully again.

I wrap my legs around his waist as he takes us both over the edge, pumping in and out of me in smooth motions. I go dizzy, climaxing as he pumps into me with hard thrusts; his release follows. I let my legs drop to the side, and he collapses across my chest, still heavily breathing. He stays inside of me, not pulling out, until we have both regained control.

When he does pull out, I miss the feel of him inside of me. I roll over, watching him climb off the bed.

"Wait there."

He walks to the attached bathroom, disposing of the condom and washing up.

When he's done, he walks back to the bed, kissing me lightly, then pulling me into his arms.

"Thank you, Angel."

* * *

For a minute, I don't remember where I am; I don't know when I fell asleep, and there's a heavy weight across my chest. Looking over, Adrian is fast asleep on his side; he looks younger in his sleep.

Good to know that wasn't all a dream.

Lifting his arm carefully, slipping out from underneath him, and stretching, I can feel every sore muscle. I am definitely going to be sore for a while.

Making my way to the bathroom, I relieve my full bladder and look in the mirror for the first time.

Oh, shit, my mom is going to kill me. The swelling doesn't seem too bad considering, a little puffy, but the purple and blue hue under my eye and down my cheek is going to be hard to hide, even with makeup. There is also bruising on my inner arm from where the asshole grabbed me; luckily, they are lighter in color and should be easy to cover.

My nipples are a little sore and red from the clamps that I would very much like to do again. Who knew sex could be that good or that anyone had multiple amazing orgasms in one night.

I smile, thinking of all the things I let him do to me throughout the night.

Tiptoeing back into the room, I grab my clothes off the floor, looking back at the bed to the gorgeous sleeping hulk in it. I walk over and kiss his lips softly, not enough to stir him, and walk out the bedroom door.

I almost don't want to leave. However, if there were ever rules on one-night stands, rule number one would be do not stay over.

Even though I know it was a one-night thing, I can't help but miss it already. He made my body feel things I could never imagine possible.

The things we did last night were straight out of a smutty romance book, and I loved every minute. It's a good thing I am not really into doing one-night stands, because there is no way any other would come close to this. I sure picked the best.

Grabbing my cell phone off the counter in the kitchen where I left it. Cursing when I see the time. Four a.m., I have to be up to help my mom in a few hours.

There are a few missed calls and texts from Lucy. Good, she can worry for a bit; she's the one who stood me up on my birthday.

Although I'm not entirely mad about it. How could I be after that night. Part of me wonders what more Adrian could show me if we had more time. Nevertheless, it was one night I will never regret.

I make my way out of the house as quietly as possible. I don't want to wake Adrian, and I don't want the awkwardness that I'm sure would come.

Luckily, my car is in the driveway with keys on the seat.

Calling Lucy as I head back toward town and my place. I don't care that it's four a.m., and she can wake her ass up.

"Where the hell are you?" Lucy says gravelly through the phone.

"Good morning to you too, princess."

"Seriously, the last thing I get from you is some random text about hooking up with a guy. Then you left me unread and didn't answer your phone."

"Well, I couldn't very well answer while being fucked silly, now could I?"

"So, you really went home with someone?" Her voice now peaked with interest—no hint of the sleep I woke her from.

"I did."

"Oh, my... Are you still with him?"

"No, I'm driving home."

"Well, hurry up; I need all the details."

"I don't know if you earned the details."

"Don't be like that; I didn't have a choice; I would have called you if I could have; you know, my dad."

I had known her not showing had something to do with her family but doesn't mean it didn't suck. I can't stay mad at her because she's been my best friend forever.

"Be there in five."

We end the call without saying goodbye.

It doesn't take long for me to make it back to my apartment; it's barely a ten-minute drive from his place to mine. I'm not the least bit surprised Lucy is waiting on the couch with two cups of hot tea when I walk in the door.

"Holy Shit, did he do that to you?"

She jumps off the couch rushing to me. It takes me a second to realize what she's talking about. My mind wasn't even thinking about the bruises, it was focused on the other sore parts of my body, ones I knew she couldn't see.

"Oh no. This happened from some other asshole." I touch my cheek, and it still stings.

"What happened?"

Walking back to the couch, I sit and take the tea she's made for me before diving into my whole night.

"First off, the asshole who did this," I say, pointing to my face. "Didn't like no for an answer, so he got a lap full of Brandy, which, as you can tell, he also didn't like very much."

"Your mom is going to freak."

"I know."

The funny thing is, we both know she isn't going to be so upset about how or why I got this way, just that it could take away from her day. Ironic since she planned her day on my birthday weekend. I give her credit for not doing it on my actual birthday, but I know that's just because she wanted to get married on a Saturday not a Friday. Lucky me.

"So, tell me about the other guy, the one you went home with. That is not like you."

"Right! But, hey, I figured what else are your twenties good for if it isn't to have some fucking fun?"

"Who are you right now?"

Laughing I wondered the same thing. Straight a student who graduated at seventeen immediately started at the local university after graduation, did three years and a ton of online courses to complete a BA in Art History six months ago. All that work to do what? Nothing?

"I figured no time like the present."

I don't know why it seems so dirty talking about it now that it's over; it could have something to do with the fact he is of age to be dating my mom, not me. So, I give Lucy a more PG version of the night, leaving out Adrian's age and the details of what we did, just telling her he rocked my world. I'll leave some things to her imagination.

"We had a good time," I say ending my retailing of the night.

"Who is he? Did he go to school with us?"

Valid question since St. George area isn't exactly massive. We lived in a smaller town just outside of the city.

"He did not go to school with us," I say vaguely.

"He works at Tipsy Roots Bar and Grill, the bar I went to last night." Not exactly a lie.

"Are you going to see him again?"

"It was a one-night stand that usually implies one night."

"So, you didn't exchange numbers or anything?" Lucy looks at me in annoyance. She stands from the couch in a huff, throwing her hands in the air. "You're impossible," she mumbles under her breath.

"What?"

"You meet someone who you say you had an immediate attraction to; he seems nice; you go have sex, and from what I can tell based off the blushing in your face was probably the best sex of your life, and you don't even get his number."

"It was a sexual, carnal attraction thing, Lucy, nothing more."

Lucy, the hopeless romantic, wouldn't understand. She's waiting on her charming fairytale prince.

I guess I would be more like that if I had her life growing up too. Her parents have been married for a long time and still like being together. They seem so happy and travel with their kids like some kind of happy little fairytale. Albeit a little controlling, like the no technology thing when with family, but a version of a fairytale nonetheless.

"Nope, sorry, Lucy, I don't even know his last name." I shrug, lifting my hands in. I don't know gesture.

"He could be the one."

Laughing, I spit out the tea I just took a sip of.

"Are you sure you aren't the one who hit your head last night?"

"Hey, it's not that funny. I'm being serious."

"Can we talk about something else besides Adrian already? Like, are you going to tell me why you couldn't even bother texting me that you weren't going to show yesterday?"

"I'm sorry; you know how it is with my dad. When he makes a plan, we have to go with him, and he won't let us bring phones. The whole living in the moment with your family thing."

"Yeah, I know. Where did you go this time?" I am still a little disappointed, but I can't really blame Lucy; her family has always been like that.

I have been friends with Lucy since middle school, and it was no different back then either. You would think as an adult, she would be over the whole family all the time, but it works for them, I guess, plus she's leaving for a year or more in a few weeks, and I know that she's going to miss her family like crazy. Although I also think part of the reason she chose to go to school in a different country is to get a little independence.

She has always had the opposite problem as I have, as she has limited independence. I have nothing but free time.

Mr. and Mrs. Smith have always treated me well when we were allowed to hang out; they are older than my parents, although that's not hard since my parents were only sixteen when they had me. The Smiths waited to start their family until they were in their thirties.

"So, what did you guys do this time?"

"Well, since Jimmy is back in town for the weekend, we went to the Red Cliffs National Conservation for some hiking."

"Oh, Jimmy's in town? I didn't know that."

"Yeah, it was a surprise visit. He was already at my parents place when I got there, or I would have given you a heads up, but I left my phone in my car, thinking it would just be a quick visit."

"You are forgiven. It just sucked not having you to celebrate with, I sat there alone for four hours."

I shrug. "I'll make it up to you tonight; we can pretend that your mom's reception is your birthday party."

"Oh, that would go over so well."

We both laugh, knowing exactly how well that would go over with my mom.

"Jimmy is going to be at the wedding too. Wink, wink."

"Lucy, how many times do I have to tell you, your twin brother and I are not, never were, and never will be a thing? Geez, I'm beginning to think you just want me with someone; it wouldn't matter to you who it is."

"I do; I'm sorry. You're just going to be all alone when I leave. I still think you should just come with me."

"I am going to miss you, but I'll be fine."

It truly was going to suck with her gone, but what kind of friend would I be if I didn't support my best friend following her dreams? Going to top-rated culinary school in Italy isn't something that everyone gets to do. I wish I could go, but she and I both know I can't afford to do that.

"Besides, I need you to leave so you can tell me all about Italy."

Getting up from the couch I yawn; I might need something stronger than tea this morning. Knowing it's far too late now to try and sleep before the wedding rehearsal and all that fun stuff.

"Any chance you want to help me look presentable?" I ask.

"Yah, go shower, and I'll do your makeup when you get out, then we can ride together over to your moms."

Adrian

The light from the wall of windows pours into the bedroom. I curse at the intrusion the light has into my dream; why hadn't I invested in black-out curtains yet?

I was having the most delicious dream of a golden-haired angel with her arms and feet bound, spread wide open by the soft rope tied to each corner of my bed, while I was eating whip cream off her delectable little body.

Licking my lips, I recall that in fact it wasn't just a dream, my Angel's soft exotic floral scent mixed with the smell of sex still lingers in the air of the room. And, indeed, at some point last night when I had insisted Emmy needed something to eat, I had rewarded her for eating the strawberries by using the rest of the whip cream to turn her into my own personal snack.

Looking around the room, I don't see any other evidence of her still being here.

When did she sneak out?

After several rounds with her, I had fallen asleep easily with her in my arms.

I shouldn't be so disappointed that she's gone. It was always just supposed to be a night of fun, but she had me doing things I didn't normally do and wanting more—things I had wanted in a long time.

I didn't bring women to my home, and I didn't let them sleep over.

I loved how she had let me push her into new experiences and loved it even more how much she enjoyed them. We had barely dabbled in anything remotely kink, yet she had responded so well.

When I was with her, it was like a part of me was whole again.

This train of thought wasn't good. It did no good to give myself any illusion there could be something more. I didn't and couldn't do more than sex; I knew that. It wouldn't be good to forget that, especially with a young thing like her; all it would do is leave her hurt and broken, just like me.

* * *

Standing on the balcony of the groom's suite and watching people scurry around setting up for the afternoon's events, I can't help but reflect on the past.

I hate weddings.

Why did I agree to be the best man?

If it was anyone other than Ryan, I wouldn't have even come to the wedding. Especially since I don't agree with him getting married in the first place. He hasn't even known this chic for more than a few months.

Not that I hated who he was marrying; in fact, I didn't know much about her. All I knew was that she was thirty-seven, previously married, had a daughter, and they met at the dog park. I wasn't even sure if Ryan knew much more about her than that.

She was probably another gold digger who recognized Ryan; she's most likely just looking for a payday. After all, he is the owner of Cresting Tech, one of the top tech companies in the country, and founder of Cresting Cars, the leading alternative fuel car and number one competitor to Tesla.

"Glad you came." Turning I see Ryan walking out the sliding door to join me.

"Of course, brother."

Not like I could really turn down my only brother.

He pats me on the back as he stands next to me.

"I know you hate weddings; trust me, I understand why. I know this can't be easy on you. It really does mean the world to me you came."

My gut wrenches, I hate how it still hurts me, still controls me, it's been twelve fucking years since Sarah was killed, killed while running from our wedding, running from me.

It's why I haven't had a real relationship since. She ran, and I still don't know why. The memories of her and that day eat away at me. I have never gotten closure. The hurt has kept me from digging for the truth all these years.

"Are you sure you want to do this?" I can't help but ask.

"When you meet her, you will understand. She's amazing." His face lights up when he talks about her.

"I just don't want to see you get hurt."

"Adrian, I'm forty years old; I built a great company and have all the money I could ever need. The one thing in life I have never had is the happiness I feel now—happiness I have never had about anything in life until I met her."

I shake my head. He's got it bad. "I came out to tell you we are doing a mini rehearsal in a minute, Joanne won't be there, obviously, but you'll get to meet her daughter since you'll be walking out together."

"Gotcha."

Great, I get to walk with the kid. Super fun day! Can we just get this shit over with and get to the open bar at the reception?

Stuck in my own head, I was hardly paying attention as the minister started going over the schedule of events, droning on about who walks when, where they will stand, and when it will start.

When a shuffle comes from behind us, turning I see a woman rushing toward us. She's looking down picking up the hem of her dress so she doesn't trip on it.

"Sorry, I had to help mom find…" she trails off. Stopping in her tracks.

Her honey brown-eyes are the size of saucers.

Fuck me! That cannot be the daughter.

She is not the little kid or preteen like I was picturing. She shakes her head and walks closer.

"*Ugh*, sorry, I was helping Mom find her necklace."

"It's okay, we were just going over timing," Ryan says to her, giving her a side hug.

I don't know what the fuck to do, run, do I say something? NO why would I say something. Like an idiot I just stand here arguing with myself.

"Adrian."

"*Huh*, what?"

Ryan is giving me that look.

"You okay?"

"Yeah, yeah all good."

He pats me on the shoulder. I'm sure assuming that whatever is bothering me is related to my past, not the beautiful angel in front of us.

"I'd like you to meet Joanne's daughter, Emmy. Emmy, this is my little brother Adrian."

She reaches out her little hand to me.

"Nice to meet you." Her hand is shaking as I take it in mine. I can see the heat rising in her cheeks already. She quickly pulls her hand back down.

She looks so fucking stunning in that lavender dress; it hugs her soft curves, accentuating her hourglassed shape; it clings to her hips, and her hair is pulled back in a loosely braided bun.

"What the heck happened to your face?" Ryan asks her, concerned.

"It's nothing. Really."

Personally, I think she did a damn good job covering it; however, I did see what it looked like before, so I have some comparison.

"We have limited time left; can we continue, please?" the minister interrupts us a bit, irritated.

"Yes, of course, my apologies," Ryan says and motions for us.

I don't hear another word said; I can't take my eyes off her, noticing she's doing her best to avoid making eye contact with me.

I can't decide if this is a curse or a blessing, so I'm going to just go with it and decide that this is going to be a good fucking day.

Emmy

"Mom, for the hundredth time, I tripped last night walking to my car, the parking lot had horrible lighting and gravel."

"I wish you'd have been a little more careful. We'll just have to make sure you stand with the other side facing the camera."

Rolling my eyes, I know she means well; she really is a great mom; she's just a little self-centered sometimes.

"Sorry, Mom."

"Can't fix it now. Oh, maybe you can pull your hair down to cover it."

"You want me to undo my hair for your pictures?" I ask incredulously.

She turns and looks at me closely, judging, and deciding if she does, in fact, want me to change my hair.

"No, I guess not; it would take away from the cut of the dress."

"Okay, Mom."

I'm just glad she didn't notice my arm or really question my explanation of how my face ended up like this. Lucy did a great job hiding most of the bruising.

"Do you know where my necklace is?"

"I don't remember seeing it," I answer.

"I need that necklace; it's something old. Grandma gave it to me; her mom gave it to her." She looks around frantically.

I know she's trying to do all the traditional stuff this time around; she really wants this one to stick, and for her, I hope it does. He seems to make her truly happy.

"Calm down, Mom. I'll find it."

Searching the bags comes up with nothing, so I end up tossing the room apart.

"Mom, are you sure you brought it here?"

"Oh, wait." She reaches down the front of her dress, pulling the necklace out of her bra.

Walking over to her, taking the necklace, I wrap the delicate chain around her neck and clasp it on her.

Giving her a hug. "You look beautiful, Mom."

Turning, she hugs me back. "Go, you're already late for the rehearsal, and you're about to ruin my makeup."

Crap I forgot about the rehearsal, sprinting down the hallway and down the stairs. Nearly falling on my face, all I need is to add a new bruise to my face; that would make my mom so happy.

Pushing the door open, I lean down, picking up the hem of my dress so I don't trip as I rush forward.

"Sorry, I had to help Mom find…"

Holy crap. Holy crap. That cannot be who I think it is standing next to Ryan.

I hadn't even realized I quit moving. Until three sets of eyes were all staring at me.

Shaking it off, I continue forward, "*Ugh*, sorry, I was helping Mom find her necklace."

"It's okay, we were just going over timing," Ryan says.

Adrian looks just as shocked to see me standing there as I do him.

What are the odds?

"Adrian."

Ryan calls his name, confirming what I already know. He doesn't reply immediately, like it took a minute for him to hear him.

"*Huh*, What?"

Ryan gives him a stern look, both concerning and disapproving. "You okay?"

"Yeah, yeah, all good," Adrian answers.

Patting Adrian on the shoulder, Ryan gestures to me. "I'd like you to meet Joanne's daughter, Emmy. Emmy, this is my little brother Adrian."

I don't know what else to do, so I reach my hand out. I can't help the shaking; I hope it's not noticeable.

"Nice to meet you." Adrian grasps my hand, giving it a slight squeeze. His touch causing the heat to blush my cheeks, great.

Pulling my hand back, I let it fall to my side.

This is going to be an interesting day.

"What the heck happened to your face?" Ryan asks, concerned.

"It's nothing. Really."

I turn slightly away to conceal the worst of it from his gaze. It's nice that he seems genuinely concerned, but I don't need him making a deal about it.

Not like I can tell him, well, I got attacked at your brother's bar, so he beat the piss out of the man who did it, then proceeded to take me to his home and fucked me all night, so if I'm not walking straight, you can take that up with him.

For a minute, he looked like he was going to press for more answers. Until we were interrupted by the minister. Thank you, God.

"We have limited time left; can we continue, please?" the minister asks with a bit of annoyance in his tone.

"Yes, of course, my apologies," Ryan says and motions for us.

I try hard to listen to what the minister is saying, I need to pay attention to anything but Adrian. I won't look in his direction.

The minister takes entirely too long to finish his expectations.

As soon as he quits talking, I turn to bolt. "Emmy," Ryan calls after me.

I don't want to stop; I don't want to look back, but it's Ryan, not Adrian, who calls my name, and I don't have a valid reason to ignore him.

Taking a deep breath in, I turn back around. Forcing a smile.

"Yeah?"

Ryan walks the short distance to me. Now that I'm standing with him, I notice the unmistakable family resemblance between the brothers. They aren't identical by any means, but they have some of the same defining features; they both have strong distinct jawlines, and Ryan keeps his shaved, unlike Adrian. They also have the same wrinkle line on their foreheads, probably caused by the stress of life. Both men have wide solid builds and are very attractive. Kind of wish I would have noticed this last night before I went home with him.

"I wanted to take a minute before the wedding to tell you how glad I am to have found your mom, and how much I look forward to getting to be a part of your life. I know you're an adult and you don't need a father figure; however, I'd really like to be someone you can count on."

"Thanks; I really appreciate that, Ryan. I'm glad my mom finally found a good one."

Can't help but wonder if he'd be feeling the same about me if he knew I had sex with his brother last night.

In my defense, I didn't know it was my soon-to-be step-uncle; Still can't imagine he'd be pleased. I'm pretty sure rule number two of having a one-night stand is not to go home with your new step dad's brother.

"I also know this probably isn't ideal for you since we kind of skipped over a big day for you with all the wedding stuff. I'd like to make that up to you."

"It's okay, Ryan."

"Here," he says nervously, reaching in the pocket of his tux.

Ryan pulls out a little black key fob, handing it to me. I look at the shiny little black plastic with a silver C on it. It's clearly a key to a Cresting automobile.

"What's this?" I ask dumbly.

"A birthday present. Happy birthday, Emmy."

"You can't just do that."

"I can. It's in the parking lot."

"Thank you."

Reaching up, I hug around his neck. He wraps his arms around me, returning the hug.

"You're welcome." He smiles.

"I better get back to Mom before she has a heart attack, wondering if everything is going to go smoothly."

He laughs. "Yeah, you better get back."

As I walk back toward the building, I look down, turning the fob in my hand. I can't believe he gifted me a car, and he knew it was my birthday.

Guess my mom talks about me more than I thought.

That's probably the nicest thing anyone has ever done for me.

Once I reach the door to head back inside, I chance a glance back out toward where Adrian was last.

Don't know what I was expecting. Was I expecting he would still be there looking at me?

Nope, his attention has already left me, guess the initial shock of seeing the girl he took home intending to fuck and forget must have worn off.

Adrian had wandered over to where the caterers were setting up a cocktail bar for guests.

A pretty brunette is rubbing her hands up his biceps. She was smiling at him, like he had said something she was interested in. Good for him.

I shouldn't care at all. So, why do I?

I just have to remind myself of what I told Lucy earlier. He was only meant to be a one-nighter, someone to have some fun with. That was even before I knew he was Ryan's brother; it should be easier now to stay away. Even if we overlooked the large age gap, things just got way more complicated. I was never supposed to see him again anyway.

Pulling out my phone I open the notes section, title a new page.

How to have a one-night stand
Never go home with a stranger from the bar.

* * *

The ceremony was beautiful; it was plain to see that my mom and Ryan cared deeply about each other.

I sure hoped that he was her one. She deserved her happy ending.

She can act a little over the top and selfish at times, but I know she has given up a lot for me over the years; she never got to be the kid. When she got pregnant at only sixteen, she chose to keep and raise me regardless of what everyone else wanted her to do, and my father wasn't any help; he was in and out the first couple of years of my life because his family tried to force him into being a father, but it didn't work out. I wasn't what he had planned or wanted in his own life.

He stopped coming around altogether around age five.

I had only seen him one other time since then. I was sixteen. I had stopped at a gas station after school, and he was at the pump across from me. He didn't even acknowledge that he saw me, even though I knew he had. His girlfriend or wife was sitting in his car, and I'm sure he didn't want to explain to her who I was.

I think he moved away after that because I hadn't seen him around since. As much as I'd like to say, it didn't bother me that he hadn't even acknowledged me; it had. It hurts knowing you weren't wanted by someone who is supposed to be there for you. Now that I'm an adult, you would think it would be easier, but still, when I think about him, it hurts, wondering why I wasn't good enough for him to want to see or know about me at all.

So even with her flaws, I was lucky to have my mom. She has always worked hard to make me feel wanted and loved; she was judged extremely hard by the people around here, and I know that hurt her, but she never showed it or took it out on me.

My grandparents are pretty great too, and, luckily, they were always around. Seeing my grandpa dressed up to walk my mom down the aisle was pretty special.

Her first wedding was in Vegas and the second at the courthouse. This is a huge upgrade for her, and my grandpa Dan clearly thought so too; he was full of pride for his little girl. Let's just hope Grandpa Dan could stay away from the open bar. He tends to enjoy a drink or two over what he should, and when he does, he tends to lose all filters.

My heart had been racing the entire ceremony, and I was thanking the almighty that I was now twenty-one and, in a short time, I could head on over to the open bar myself. I wasn't worried about drinking too much. I didn't much like the feeling of actually being drunk. However, if I was going to have to deal with being this close to Adrian all night, I needed a few drops.

I would have to be blind not to appreciate how good Adrian looked in that suit; he was portraying every ounce of his masculinity.

He must have spent a pretty penny at the tailor to get that thing made to fit him like a glove.

Ugh, I was not going to spend all night thinking about him. I mentally chastised myself again.

I finally got a reprieve from my thoughts of Adrian when the minister finished off the ceremony.

"I now pronounce you husband and wife; you may now kiss the bride."

Thank the heavens.

One more uncomfortable walk back the opposite way, linked arms with Adrian, and I'll be free.

I can do this.

He walks over to me, offering me his arm. I take it like I'm supposed to. Why did he have to smell so good? It's intoxicating, and his mix of cologne and body wash is clean and sexy.

I feel like my heart is going to pound out of my chest as we walk back down the aisle.

"You look incredible, my angel," he whispers so low I barely hear him.

I don't dare look up at him; I am doing all I can to hold my nerves together as it is, and if I look into those eyes, I'll be a puddle.

Stiffening, pulling my hand free of his arm as soon as we hit the doorway, bee-lining it out of there, heading straight to the Champaigne.

I manage to put down two glasses before my mom comes up behind me. I probably should pace myself, but damn, this night is uncomfortable as hell.

"Emmy, what are you doing? We still have pictures to take."

I hate the look she is giving me; it's the same look she gives her dad—the pure look of disappointment. I had worked so hard growing up not to get that look from her.

"Now?" I sigh.

"Yes now! What has gotten into you?"

"Sorry, Mom."

I set down my empty glass and follow her to the area for the pictures. Thankful for the little liquid courage in me, even if it did disappoint my mom a little.

Adrian

"How old did you say your new wife is again?" I ask Ryan

"Huh, thirty-seven, why?" He looks at me questioningly as we wait for the photographer to snap another picture of the two of us.

"Her daughter just looks older, is all."

"She is; she's twenty-one; Joanne had her at sixteen."

Oh, thank the heavens, she hadn't lied to me, I didn't cross that line, that I would have never forgiven myself for.

"And you're sure she isn't just after your money?"

Ryan looks like he wants to hit me for that one.

"I'm sure, not that it's any of your business brother, but she insisted on a prenup."

That did earn brownie points in my book.

"I would like it if you wouldn't think of your new sister-in-law as the enemy and actually try to be in our lives."

"Yeah, okay, I'll do my best."

"Now for the group." The photographer's chipper voice commands as she starts positioning everyone; the bride's parents are here and where ours aren't. She moves Emmy to stand on the side next to me to even out the bodies.

I can hear her intake of breath as the photographer pushes her in a little closer.

That makes me grin like a Cheshire cat.

That's right, Angel; I love how she reacts when I'm near; too bad, I won't be exploring more of her limits.

I can't help myself though and let my hand graze against her exposed back as everyone splits apart, finally done with pictures.

She visibly shivers as goosebumps show on her skin. I know she has been purposely ignoring me, and damn if it doesn't drive me crazy, on multiple occasions I had to force myself to think of something else, or I'd have had to explain to Ryan why the front of my slacks were tented.

"Excuse me," she says to her mom and Ryan, who are only feet in front of us. Emmy steps passed them, heading into the building where the suites everyone used while we got ready are.

I just shrug when Ryan looks back over his shoulder at me with a questioning look.

"She has been so weird today," Joanne comments to Ryan.

"Maybe she isn't feeling very well; she did hit her head," Ryan adds.

"I would assume she probably has a headache or something; with a hit like that, she probably has a minor concussion," I remark.

I feel a little guilty about all we did last night. I'm such an asshole; a good man would have looked after her and made sure she was okay. I am not the good man; I pushed her, and fucked her until she was completely worn out. Fuck, just another reason I need to stay away from her.

They both look at me questioningly.

"I mean, from the looks of it, it looks like it was a pretty bad hit." I try to cover my mistake. I don't know what she actually told them.

"True, it did look pretty bad. I still don't get how she tripped and fell into her car. I sure hope it wasn't from drinking," Joanne says with concern in her eyes.

Ryan puts his arm around her waist, gripping her to his side and squeezing her reassuringly. "We will make sure she's good," he says sweetly.

Hmm, she tripped into her car, so that's what she told them. Why are they so concerned about her drinking anyway? She didn't seem like a big drinker to me.

"What makes you think she was drunk when she hit her head?" I ask.

"She was out at some bar last night, then she fell into her car badly enough to smack her head, which means she didn't even try to catch herself. Indicating she was intoxicated. Plus, alcoholism runs in the family," Joanne says, with sorrow or regret in her eyes.

"I don't think your daughter is an alcoholic. Trust me, I know alcoholics."

"Did you know she was at the bar when I went to get her for the pictures? She had two empty glasses in front of her already," Joanne says, looking at Ryan.

"Nerves, maybe you think this wedding isn't stressful for her too?" I say defensively. Not sure why I feel the need to defend her.

"Maybe, but…"

"Let's go; there are people waiting at the reception. Emmy will be fine, love," Ryan interrupted her, and I was thankful I didn't need to get in an argument with Joanne and have to explain how I knew she wasn't drinking when she hit her head.

Ryan kisses his new wife at her temple and guides her over to where the reception is starting. Glaring back at me before focusing on the people in front of him.

I don't know why I was letting it bug me so bad that they had this picture of Emmy in their heads, like she was just going around getting sloshed or something. She had barely touched the drink last night.

* * *

People milled around, congratulating the newlyweds.

I was sitting at one of the round tables, watching the people coming and going from the venue.

Emmy had only come down to the reception about thirty minutes ago, just in time to watch the cake cut and the couple's first dance.

I found myself seeking her out on several occasions as I sat there.

The reception was being held outside; luckily, there was a slight breeze that kept the warm summer air bearable. The tables were set up a few feet apart with cream-colored cloths on them, fake flicker light candles and gardenias in the center, and string lights draped around the open canopy. It was even complete with a square floor area for the dancing.

"Hey, Adrian, you promised me a dance earlier." The feathery voice of Tonya says taking me away from my most recent search of the area.

"I did?" I look at her questioningly.

Tonya was a beautiful woman, long brunette hair, deep brown eyes, bronzed complexion, and a body most men would go crazy over.

I had known her for a long time. She was friends with both Ryan and me; we had all met while in college at Oregon State years ago.

I knew she was hoping she and I would become a thing, at least until I fell for her cousin Sarah, who had come to visit her one weekend.

Tonya and I had never been romantically involved, and we never would be; however, that didn't stop her from trying.

I'll give her credit, though she mostly backed off when I got with Sarah except for the one time she tried to get me to leave Sarah, and she did give it what she considers a reasonable amount of time before showing interest again after Sarah's accident, even though there is no reasonable amount of time in my book. If we hadn't been friends for so long, I wouldn't even give her the time of day. She was harmless, though.

"Well, maybe you didn't, but you should have." She pouts.

Looking around, I notice Emmy is on the dance floor in the arms of some skinny blond kid, with a big smile on her face as he twirled her around to the fun beat of "Wanna Be Startin' Somethin" by Michael Jackson, played.

"Sure, why not?" I say to Tonya, who's eyes light up, it was an excuse for me to be closer to Emmy.

She grabs my arm as I stand and rushes me to the floor before I can change my mind.

Just as we hit the dance floor, the song shifts to a slow love ballad. The last thing I wanted to do was slow dance with Tonya.

Tonya wastes no time wrapping around me, getting as close as she can. I reluctantly hold onto her as we sway to the music. I look around the dance floor and see Emmy still dancing with the blond kid. His hand is resting just above her ass, where the fabric ends to her backless dress. For the first time tonight, her eyes meet mine, and it takes all my control not to dump Tonya on her ass as she lays her head on my shoulder.

Emmy looks at me, taking in Tonya trying to share my skin. Despite my efforts to keep her at a distance, she's all handsy. I see something flash in Emmy's eyes before she quickly looks away—jealousy maybe. Gawds I hoped it was, because I know that I hate that kid's hands on her, and it is taking all self-control for me not to go there and grab her out of his arms.

Turning away from me, she looks up at her dance partner, whispering something in his ear. They stop dancing, and he grabs her hand, leading her off the floor.

I want to follow, but I can't without causing a scene. The song drags on, and I hate every minute of it.

I have to remind myself, Emmy isn't mine; she was only meant to be a one-night stand.

So, why did my body say otherwise? Why did I want to go rip the arm off that kid, a kid she was clearly comfortable with?

Peeling Tonya away from me as the song ends and a more modern song starts to play.

I am not getting stuck for another three minutes with her.

She tries to protest, but luckily, I'm saved by some poor sap who doesn't know what he's getting into asks if he can take this next dance.

I gladly hand her over and walk off the dance floor.

Weaving through the tables that separate the dance area from the bar side of the set-up I see Emmy standing, talking to a girl and the kid she was dancing with.

Walking toward them, I notice the kids hand go to Emmy's face, where the bruise is. He's looking it over, very comfortable touching her, and it makes my blood boil. If she had a fuckin boyfriend, she should have said something last night. I hate fuckin cheaters.

"How did you say you got this again?" the kid asks.

"Tripped on some loose gravel on my way to the car last night."

The girl with them rolls her eyes at Emmy; clearly, she doesn't believe her lame story.

I walk closer. Seeing me, she steps back from the kid.

"Maybe you should talk to the bar owner to fix that gravel, liability issues, and all." I joke.

"Yeah, maybe you could sue or something," the girl says.

"Lucy, seriously," Emmy says, giving her a what-the-fuck look.

"Kidding." She puts up her hands in defeat.

The girl, who I now know is Lucy, looks at me, offering her hand.

"We haven't met; I'm Lucy, bestie to Emmy on the bride's side. You must belong on Ryan's side."

Taking her hand, I shake it lightly.

"Adrian Montgomery, brother of the groom."

Lucy looks from me to Emmy and back. "Nice to meet you, Adrian." She puts a little extra emphasis on my name.

I don't miss the blush that has crept up Emmy's face for the second time tonight.

"This is my brother Jimmy. He's in med school," Lucy says, nudging Jimmy in the side.

"Nice to meet you too." I offer my hand, gripping him a little harder than I should have.

"Yeah, you too," he says dryly.

"I saw you guys out on the dance floor earlier; you make a cute couple," I say.

Almost in unison, they both reply, "We are not a couple."

Lucy laughs. "Told you guys, you would be cute together."

"Not happening, sis; no offense, Emmy."

"None taken." She smiles.

I can't help but be relieved at their response. Not that it should matter to me in the slightest. I have to keep reminding myself that she is off limits and I don't do relationships.

"I tried," Lucy says with a laugh.

The night ticks away, and I find myself falling into easy conversation with Emmy and her friends.

I've learned Lucy is a chef and will be on her way to Italy in a couple weeks. Jimmy is in his second year at med school, and Emmy graduated highschool early and has already completed her BA.

I can't help but be impressed.

"I think I'm going to head out. It was good meeting you," Jimmy says, and excuses himself.

I hadn't realized how close Emmy and I were standing now until Emmy went to turn away and bumped into me.

"Sorry," I say, grabbing her arm so she doesn't lose her balance.

"No problem."

She takes a step back from me, trying to hide the heat that I know she felt from my touch—the same heat that's now tingling in my fingers from the feel of her soft skin under mine.

"You'll have to excuse me; I'm a bit of a klutz as of late," she says softly, closing her eyes for a brief second as she takes in a breath.

I don't know what comes over me, but I need to be closer to her again; I need to feel her in my arms.

"Would you like to dance?" I dare ask her.

Emmy looks at me a little shocked that I would ask; it's not like we haven't been standing here together for the past hour at least.

"Sure," her answer comes out a little hesitant.

I take her hand and walk her toward the dance floor. I watch her closely; she seems nervous, not at all like the confident girl I had in my bed last night. I guess I'm just a masochist, because this is pure torture being with her and not being able to do what I truly want to her. I should feel bad for thinking of all the ways I want to take her. I should, but I don't.

"It's perfectly normal for people to dance at a wedding," I say jokingly trying to ease some of her nerves.

We have barely made it to the dance floor when Emmy stops me, placing a hand on my arm.

"I'm sorry, I-I just can't." She pauses, looking around like someone is watching us. "I still have a little headache; I think I'm going to turn in," she adds.

Not giving me time to talk to her out of leaving, she hurries away from me; I don't follow her as she walks away.

She probably doesn't want her mom to see her dancing with me; I should be worried about that too, but spending time with her seems to be the only thing I can focus on.

Lucy must have noticed the way I was watching her; out of nowhere, she was next to me.

Clearing her throat, he says, "*Ehmm.*"

Turning I look at Lucy. For the first time tonight, I get a good look at the girl. My attention has been focused on Emmy; Lucy has the same blonde hair as her brother Jimmy; it's a lighter color blonde, not as golden yellow as Emmy's. Lucy's hair is cut in a short A-line style, reminding me of a blonde Victoria Beckham; she's also a few inches taller than Emmy.

I smile at her. "Yes?"

"Do you happen to be thee Adrian?"

I look around to see who is close and motion for her to walk further away from the dance area where most of the guests are mingling.

"*Hmm*, that depends; I am the Adrian Montgomery," I say when we are closer to the end of the bar area again. Clearly, she told her about me, but I don't know how much, and the last thing I want to do is add to Emmy's clearly tensed mood.

"Funny," Lucy says not at all amused.

"You will have to elaborate on the 'thee' you are referring to."

Lucy places her hands on both sides of her hips.

"You know, rock her world one nighter," she whispers, clearly embarrassed to be asking yet still standing as if she is pissed off at me.

I lean down, getting closer to Lucy. I am a little amused.

"Do tell me more," I say sinfully.

Lucy drops her hands. "Never mind. Must be a coincidence." She practically huffs.

Just as I am about to toy with the girl more, Ryan taps my shoulder.

"Hey, Adrian, Emmy's head seems to be giving her trouble; she is wanting to leave. I was hoping you wouldn't mind taking her home, and maybe keeping an eye on her for a few days while we are gone."

I would love to take her home and spend more time with her again. Not that I can exactly tell him that.

"You want me to stay and watch your wife's adult daughter?"

He looks a little uncomfortable about asking, "Could you please? Joanne and I would feel a lot better about leaving if we know someone is looking after her."

"Sure, I can check in on her while you're gone."

"Thank you. It means a lot."

"I'm still going to be here for a few weeks," Lucy interrupts.

"Oh, yes, of course. Sorry, Lucy. I know you have a lot to get ready before you go and didn't want you to have to worry about watching over Emmy."

"You know I don't mind."

"Of course not," Ryan says apologetically.

"I have to stay in town a little longer to go over some of the bar stuff anyway, so I don't mind checking in on her here and there giving you a break," I offer casually.

"If you guys are done discussing who you think is going to babysit me, I'm leaving," Emmy says continuing to walk past us.

"Oh, and Lucy, spend time with Jimmy and your family, I will be fine on my own. I don't need a sitter," Emmy says sharply.

Ryan looks a little sad; I know he's just trying to show her he cares.

"Emmy, let me at least drive you," I call after her.

She stops pivoting on her heels. "You could even stay at my house for a couple days until you're feeling hundred percent," I add as she stares at me dead in the face.

"No thanks." Her tone was short and clipped. She looks like a coiled snake, ready to strike.

"I know you just met him, but I promise he's not a complete ass. Besides, your mom and I would feel much better if you weren't alone."

"No offense, Ryan, but I have been taking care of myself for quite a while. I'm good."

I watch as the color from her face drains immediately, regretting saying that the second it comes out of her mouth.

I don't know her well, but Emmy doesn't seem like the type to be rude like this on purpose.

A small gasp comes from behind me, turning to look. Joannes standing two feet behind us, her hands go to her face as she tries to cover her hurt. Ryan wraps an arm around her, pulling her into him protectively. Kissing the top of her head.

"It's okay, love. She didn't mean that."

"Mom, I'm so sorry. I really didn't. I don't know what's gotten into me."

Emmy takes a step forward, placing a hand on her mom's arm, then drops it back down again.

"I am sorry, Mom. That came out wrong. It's the headache; it's making me grouchy. I'm sorry," she apologizes over and over.

Joanne calms down and shakes it off. "It's okay. I know you didn't mean it. Go get some rest."

Joanne hugs her daughter, kissing her on the cheek.

"I'll see you when we get back in a couple weeks."

"Okay, Mom." She hugs her tightly.

"Let me at least take you home," I offer again.

Emmy nods in response.

Emmy

I had to get away from him. Even though we had been getting along and the conversations flowed easily with my friends, I was wound up tight, like a jack in the box, ready to pop at any second.

The closer we got to the dance floor, the tighter I was being wound.

I didn't know how long I could be this close to him.

Reminders of how it felt to have his hands on me, I wanted it again.

I know I shouldn't, but I keep thinking of how amazing it was to be with him last night. He was so gentle with me. The images of how sexual and intimate we had been less than twenty-four hours ago, floating through my brain.

My head was pounding, and the stress of everything waying on me.

Walking away from him, I scanned the crowd, making sure no one was watching us. It had been stupid to spend so much time with him tonight.

I was a little worried to leave him, knowing Lucy, she is going to try and hunt him down for answers. She didn't know he was the same guy I was talking about, but I watched the way she had eyed him several times tonight, and I knew she was suspicious, besides how many Adrians did we have around here.

I'm glad I hadn't gone into more detail about the things we had done, that would be a whole other level of embarrassment I didn't want to deal with right now.

After passing by Mom and Ryan and letting them know I wasn't feeling the best, I walked inside into the bathroom to splash some water on my face and check on the bruises on my face everyone was fussing over.

The beautiful brunette that I had seen hanging on Adrian all night was putting on more lipstick and talking on her phone when I walked in.

Her perfume overpowered the small space, and I can't help but wonder who would like to smell that all night.

I wasn't trying to eavesdrop on her conversation, but the space isn't large, so it's not hard to miss.

"Yeah, I don't think I'll be back tonight. I plan on staying at Adrian's place," she says to whoever she is talking to.

I turn on the water, lightly splash my face, and fix myself as best I can.

She giggles. "Yeah, you know how he is; he couldn't keep his dirty hands off me. Just like it was before Sarah," she says.

"Oh, he'll forget her name when we are done tonight; I'll remind him what he's been missing out on," giggling again at whatever the person on the other end of her call said.

I feel sick to my stomach. I need to get out of here.

Turning off the water, I walk out of the bathroom.

Finding my mom and Ryan again, I let them know I'm definitely not feeling great and headed out.

I have to head back inside to get my stuff from the room. *Ugh,* the brunette walks out of the bathroom as I walk into the hall. Ignoring her, I continue to walk past her.

"Hey girl," she shouts.

I turn and look at her. "Are you talking to me?"

"Of course."

"Can I help you with something?" I ask, not really in the mood to talk to her.

"I saw you with my man Adrian earlier; let me give you a little advice. Stay away from him."

Her Adrian?

"I'm afraid I don't know what you're talking about."

She steps closer to me. "Don't play dumb with me, little girl; I saw how you were all over him. He's mine; he always has been, always will be."

I step back, holding my hands out in front of me, hoping she will calm down. Not sure what she was seeing because I am pretty sure I avoided contact with him as much as possible.

"I don't know who you are, but you don't know what you're talking about."

"Sarah thought the same thing: don't get in my way." She points a finger at me, pressing it into my chest.

What the fuck? Slapping her hand away from me.

"I have no idea what you are talking about, you crazy bitch," I say and storm off.

I quickly grab my bag and head out to leave. I am so worked up from her and from this damn throbbing in my head.

I wanted to let Lucy know I was leaving, and it only adds to my annoyance when I see she is talking to Ryan and Adrian.

The closer I get, I can overhear them talking about who's going to babysit me.

Really?

"I'm still going to be here for a few weeks." I hear Lucy offer.

"Oh, yes, of course. Sorry, Lucy. I know you have a lot to get ready before you go and didn't want to have you watching over Emmy."

"You know I don't mind."

"Of course not," Ryan says apologetically to Lucy.

"I have to stay in town a little longer to go over some of the bar stuff anyway, so I don't mind checking in here and there and giving you a break," Adrian adds.

And I want to puke; he is the last person I want to be with right now. What a fuckin player. What was I expecting? He picked me up from a bar minutes after meeting me.

"If you guys are done discussing who you think is going to babysit me, I'm leaving." I am annoyed, and I don't try to hide it in my tone.

"Oh, Lucy, spend time with Jimmy and your family. I will be fine on my own. I don't need a sitter."

Ryan looks at me with sadness on his face. I don't know what he's trying to prove; he doesn't need to try so hard. I don't expect him to be my dad or care.

"Let me at least drive you," Adrian calls after me. I stop walking, pivoting so that I am facing him. "You could even stay at my house for a couple days until you're feeling hundred percent," he adds. Looking him dead in the eyes.

"No thanks." I can't keep the anger from my tone.

"I know you just met him, but I promise he's not a complete ass. Besides, your mom and I would feel much better if you weren't alone."

"No offense, Ryan, but I have been taking care of myself for quite a while. I'm good."

I regret my words and tone the second it comes out of my mouth. It's not his, my mom's or even Adrian's fault I'm in such a foul mood. I can't take the look on my mom's face, who I didn't even notice sneaking up behind them as we were talking.

A small gasp escapes her, and she brings her hands to her as she tries to cover her hurt.

Ryan pulls her to him protectively. Kissing the top of her head. "It's okay, love. She didn't mean that."

"He's right I really didn't; I was just in a mood."

"Mom, I'm so sorry. I really didn't; I don't know what's gotten into me." I place a hand on her arm, then drop it back down again.

"I am sorry, Mom. That came out wrong. It's the headache; it's making me grouchy. I'm sorry." I try to apologize over and over.

My mom finally calms down a little and shakes it off. "It's okay; I know you didn't mean it. Go get some rest." She hugs me and kisses me on the cheek. I can tell she is still hurt.

"I'll see you when we get back in a couple weeks," she adds.

"Okay, Mom." I hug her back tightly.

"Let me at least take you home," Adrian offers again.

I nod. I don't have the energy to argue, and I don't want to hurt my mom or Ryan any more. I feel like a complete ass.

"I can do it if you want," Lucy suggests.

"It's okay; I know your parents were excited to have you both at home this weekend."

Lucy hugs me.

"We will talk later," I tell her I really do need to lay down.

In the parking lot, I see the shiny new red Cresting. I'm a little pissed; I don't even get to drive my new car.

I can't believe Ryan really got me this as a birthday present, and I showed him thanks by being a complete bitch at their wedding.

I take a closer look at the car as I wait for Adrian to grab his stuff out of the groom's room.

When did my life get so complicated? I squeeze the bridge of my nose. Leaning back against my new car.

This parking lot has better lighting, and I know I'm in a safe place, but I'm still a little jumpy the longer I wait. What the hell is taking him so long?

I just wanted to lay down and sleep. Stupidly and selfishly. I wanted Adrian to hold me as I did.

Pulling out my phone I added to the note earlier.

How to have a one-night stand
Never go home with a stranger from the bar.
Never develop feelings for the guy.

Sighing, I close my phone. When I'm confronted with exactly what has been taking him so long, walking out of the building is Adrian and the Brunette bitch from earlier; she is hanging on his shoulder, his arm around her back, and his hands on her waist.

Why am I so stupid?

She giggles as they walk out. I can see the red lipstick on his face and neck. The breeze drifts her strong perfume over to me, and I want to throw up.

Fuck this shit, I am leaving. If he thinks for a second I would get in a car with that psycho, he's wrong. I know I'm being irrational; he isn't mine; he made that clear from the beginning, and so did I. Not to mention he's older than my mom, and his brother just married her, making Adrian completely off limits.

I need sleep, so I can wake up from this nightmare. In less than twenty-four hours, my life has gone completely out of whack.

Pulling out the shiny new key fob, I auto start the Cresting. Walking from the passenger side, I had been leaning on over to the driverside.

"What are you doing, Emmy?" Adrian yells across the parking lot.

"Leaving," I yell back.

I probably shouldn't be driving right now, but what other option do I have? Stay here and wait with him and that psycho; no thanks.

The brunette giggles again. "Let her go, baby; she's nobody."

"Let go, Tonya." Adrian grits out. I can see he's struggling to get out of her grip to get to me. I don't care; I climb in and reverse out of the stall.

I watch in my rear-view mirror as Tonya is dropped to the pavement, and Adrian sprints after my car. I glance one more time in my mirror before putting it in drive and hitting the throttle.

The look of hurt crosses his face. What did he have to be hurt by? He made his priorities and intentions clear all along.

I was the stupid one who let my emotions get all mixed in; he was a bar hook up, a one-night stand, nothing more, and I'm sure he was being so nice earlier to make sure I didn't make some kind of scene in front of his brother. I'm sure he wasn't thrilled to see me today either, but the difference is, he isn't all hung up on it like I am.

The sooner I get away from him and remember that, the better I'll be.

Between the headache and my thoughts, I'm not really paying attention. I passed the road to my apartment three turns ago. Not really knowing what to do, I just want to be alone. I just want to go home and wake up tomorrow, forgetting all about last night.

If I go home, though, there is a chance Lucy could come home, and I really don't want to talk about anything.

I feel so childish. I knew I was overreacting.

But after spending hours with him standing so close to me—the glances—how easily he talked with my friends, it just felt like it could be more.

It was clearly wishful thinking that the chemistry between us wasn't one-sided.

* * *

I was exhausted. I gave up arguing with myself after twenty minutes of driving to nowhere and headed back to my apartment. I needed my bed, and I needed this day to be over with. I needed this whole weekend to be over with.

Pulling in my parking stall, I curse when I shut off the car. Across the pathway in front of my door is a very angry-looking Adrian.

His arms are crossed across his chest. Leaning against my door. He's still wearing his suit shirt and pants but has lost the jacket.

I can't help thinking how out of place his big, muscled frame looks standing there. My dumpy apartment is not a place you would picture someone like him.

Adrian

The hell this girl was putting me through—she is going to pay for it when I get my hands on her. I'm tempted to lay her over my lap and redden her pretty little ass.

Although I am relieved when she finally pulls in and parks her car.

What the hell was she thinking?

After shoving an intoxicated Tonya into a taxi cab, I had to run back into the wedding, asking Ryan what the tracker on Emmy's car was, without Joanne hearing.

Then I had to explain to an upset Ryan that I had let her get in a car and drive away, not an easy thing to explain to my brother since none of her attitude toward me would make any sense to him, not to mention the mess with Tonya. I still don't get why she was even here tonight; she was a major pain in my ass. I know we were all friends once, but did Ryan really forget the hell she put her own cousin through?

It wasn't my concern anymore, however, Emmy was.

Once Ryan had finally handed over her apartment address and the info for the Cresting's built-in tracker, I set out to find her.

Only to be completely frustrated because she just kept driving around. Twenty fucking minutes of her driving around with no apparent rhyme or reason.

I hadn't wanted to spook her, so I followed at a safe distance for most of that time until I realized she was finally headed back toward her apartment.

I had flipped around and drove as fast as I could to her place in order to make it here before her.

From where I am leaning against her light wood door, I watched her face and could see that she was clearly struggling with her decision. I'm sure she is contemplating whether or not to put the car in reverse and flee from me again or to get out of her car to confront me.

I would think it was adorable; if I wasn't so damn mad at her for taking off in the first place.

After a minute, she steps out of her car, walking toward me.

Pushing off from the door so I'm standing tall in front of her.

"Why are you here? Where's your girlfriend?" she says venomously.

I can't help the low chuckle. Was that what this was about? Was she jealous?

"What have you been doing?" I ask.

"None of your business."

She pushes past me to reach her door. Grabbing her shoulder, twisting her so she has to face me. I push her backward; her back hits the door; it creeks but doesn't budge. I step closer to her, leaning down, grabbing the nape of her neck with one hand, and tilting her chin up with the other.

Her eyes go big as she looks at me, and she takes in a breath. I don't know what comes over me, but I crush my lips to hers. Within seconds, she relaxes into me, taking my hard kiss and returning it with the same need I have. Her hands wrap around my neck and into my hair.

Not wanting to break away from her but knowing I have to, I let my rational thinking take over as I pull back, breaking the kiss, and letting go of her.

She lets out a small whimper at the loss.

"You scared the shit out of me," I admit.

Only one other person in my life has ever made me feel emotions the way Emmy does, and even then, I was never so out of control with my emotions, not the way I am with her.

When I watched her get in that car and drive off tonight, I lost it. Part of me wasn't only thinking of Emmy in that moment; it was all about the emotions it brought up.

It took me back to the day I lost Sarah. The day she left me. I'll never forget the look on her face when she said no instead of "I do." She looked broken right before she ran out on our wedding.

I chased after her, but she got in that car and never looked back. To this day, I still don't know what changed her mind; what made her look so broken. Whatever it had been, I was sure it was just a misunderstanding, something we could figure out; after all, I had loved her, wanted to be with her, wanted a life with her, and we could have worked out anything.

Sarah never gave me that chance, though, and the last time I saw her alive was when she got in that car.

The witness reports say she drifted over the line and tried to correct it, over correcting, causing her car to spin and flip, which made it roll down into a ditch embankment. She must have been crying and not paying attention to her speed or the road.

I shake my head to bring me from spiraling in the memories.

Stepping back, adding distance between Emmy and myself.

My heart is pounding. The feelings all this has stirred up, this is one major reason I don't do relationships. There are too many fucking feelings involved.

Emmy looks at me.

"You okay?" she asks softly.

"No, you fuckin left," I say louder than I meant too.

All this extra shit in my head right now isn't her fault.

"You came out with that bitch draped all over you; the message received loud and clear," she says angrily.

"It's not what you're clearly thinking it was, Angel." I say in a calmer tone.

"Do you call all your bitches that?"

"Listen, you have it all wrong. Can we go in and talk, please?"

Her neighbors are close, and I'm sure the walls aren't that thick in this place. The last thing we need tonight is the police called.

She opens the door and steps inside, leaving the door open behind her.

I'll take that as a yes.

I walk into her tiny apartment, closing the door behind me. The door leads directly into the living space; a small kitchen is off to the side, with the counter open to the living space.

Emmy flips on the lights, making it easier to look around the space. She has a coffee table and sofa in the small space, two bar stools at the counter, and no kitchen table. The place is clean and tidy, and large, colorful art hangs on the walls. The art is in major contrast to the pale color of the walls, counters, and white fridge.

"Okay, let's talk. Want to tell me why you didn't bother to tell me about Tonya?"

"Excuse me?" I don't know what she wanted me to tell her.

"Look, I wasn't under the impression that we were going to be a thing, but I don't like being lied to."

"I never lied to you."

"So, Tonya threatening me to stay away from her man was just for fun, then, a joke, part of a game you play?" Making the quotations with her fingers as she says her man.

"You talked to Tonya?" I look at her in utter shock and disbelief.

Emmy throws her hand up in a way of dismissing what I'm saying.

"More like, I was accosted by her in the hall. After hearing her tell someone else she was spending the night with you like before."

"I have no idea what you're talking about."

I want to reach out and pull her to me, but she shrugs me off, walking into the kitchen, Emmy grabs herself a glass, filling it with water, and grabbing a small pill bottle out of another cabinet. She pops two pills.

"Look, I don't have the energy to hash out shit with you; I really do have a headache, and I'm exhausted."

Walking up to her, I run the back of my fingers down the side of her cheek.

She sighs and leans into me.

"Please don't. I can't deal with how you make me feel." Placing a hand on my chest.

She drops her hand from my chest, looking deflated. She walks and sits on the couch, pulling her feet up to her chest.

She looks so small and so vulnerable; this is where I should dismiss myself and leave.

Instead I walk over to the small couch.

"Can I sit?"

"Sure."

Taking the spot next to her, I leave some space between us.

"First off, you were the one gone when I woke up," I begin, "no note, nothing, just gone. Then you were the one who chose to ignore me half the day." I add trying not to let it show how much it bugged me.

"Oh, yes, cuz I could just be like, oh, hey, Ryan. Yup we already met; he's your brother you say; yeah, I fucked him."

"Don't be crude, Emmy; it doesn't fit you."

Yet, I can't help the small smile her words bring out. She's such a contrast to herself sometimes. I should probably be worried, but I'm not; I fucking love it.

"I'm not being crude. Honestly, I don't know what to be. I was fine leaving this morning, thinking I wouldn't have to see you again. I wouldn't have to admit how your touch sends heat through my entire body and how the things we did excited me."

Well, shit, if what she was saying wasn't exactly how I was feeling too, I want to touch her again. I want to show her just how much she affects me too. I know this is a fucked-up situation, but its not that bad. Right?

The demons that still live in my head won't let me tell her that, though; they won't let me tell her I feel the same way, that just being next to her has me wanting more, that I can't get enough of her that all I have wanted to do all day was be with her.

So, we sit in silence instead.

The silence seems to drag on for several minutes until Emmy looks up at me and asks something I never imagined she would.

"Who is Sarah?"

The breath leaves my lungs, like she's punched me in the gut.

"Where did you hear that name?"

Adjusting, she crosses her legs and sits up straighter.

"Tonya said her name a few times on the call, and then when she confronted me in the hall, she said that I better stay out of her way because you were hers. Then she said something about Sarah, thinking she could take you too or something like that."

Rage builds up in me as I listen to her tell me about what Tonya said and did.

Thinking back to the day before Sarah and I were supposed to get married, I was at my buddy's house for a little pre-wedding bachelor thing with a few of the guys. We had been drinking, and Tonya showed up. She had tried to get me to take her into the bedroom. I declined her advances and had opted to go to bed early, alone. But now I was wondering if she told Sarah something more had happened between us. Could that be why Sarah left? Did she think I slept with her cousin?

"That fuckin bitch," I say through gritted teeth.

"Sarah was supposed to be my wife; she was Tonya's cousin." Anger is evident in my tone; it rolls through my body.

"Supposed to be?" she asks meekly.

I stand from the couch and begin pacing the small room. I don't talk about my past to many people.

I don't know why she would be any different, but I have a need to tell Emmy everything. I need her to know the truth.

So, I tell her everything, including the accident that took Sarah from me forever.

After telling her about Sarah, I filled her in on how Tonya ended up in my arms on the way out of the wedding tonight, how I had run into her stumbling in the hall, and I had called her a cab. I was only trying to get her out to the cab when she started kissing all over me. I had to stop her a few times, which is why it took us so long to get outside.

Looking back now, I wonder if it was all a ruse.

By the time I was done talking, I had practically worn a hole in her cheap carpet.

There it was—my whole story, now out there. I have never told anyone everything before, especially not a girl I was fucking.

Emmy wasn't just a girl I had fucked though, or at least I didn't want her to be. That thought also scares the shit out of me; I haven't wanted to be more with anyone in over twelve years.

I turn to face her, not knowing what to expect. She seems to be taking it all pretty well; I have to give her credit. She didn't interrupt me once.

I was immediately relieved when I looked at her, and she didn't have the look most people who knew about Sarah did—that look of pity.

It's a look. I had gotten a lot for the first couple years after Sarah's death, and I fucking hated that look.

"I was only nine when all that happened," Emmy says in astonishment.

I couldn't help the deep laugh that came out of me.

"Oh sorry." She blushes.

"No, it's good. Thank you." I am glad she could take the anger and sadness inside of me and calm it down.

She did have a big point, though. I had lived an entire lifetime before she was even out of grade school; there was no way I was going to make this work.

Emmy yawns. Making me feel extra guilty for adding more on top of her already shit day.

Walking to stand in front of her, I lean down and rub a thumb across her cheek, stopping at her lips. Lips, I want to press mine against again.

"You need to get some rest, Angel."

"Sorry, I'm so tired and a little sore. I had incredible sex multiple times last night." She blinks at me sheepishly, smiling.

Lifting her off the couch, I walk her down the hall, carrying, her bridal style as if we just walked across the threshold.

"Which one's yours?" I ask when there are two rooms at the end of the small hall.

"That one." She points to the door on our left with her foot.

Pushing the door open, letting the hall light cast a glow into the room.

I can't see the room well with only the dim hall lighting. However, I can make out a dresser on the wall near the door, a bed in the center of the room across from where we just walked in, and a nightstand to one side of the bed.

Walking toward the bed, I need to set her down, so I can pull the covers back from the bed.

"On your feet, Angel."

I don't release her completely until I know she can stand on her own.

When I lift my hands from her skin, I notice her shiver, goosebumps covering her arms.

I pull the cover down, so she walks toward the bed, standing and waiting.

"Strip," I say.

She does as I ask, pulling the small straps down her arms. I had pictured that dress coming off all night, just in a slightly different way than this.

It slides down her body, leaving her exposed.

"You naughty girl." I knew she wasn't wearing a bra, as the dress had a built-in one with the way it was cut; a normal one would never work. However, had I known she wasn't wearing any panties either, I wouldn't have made it through that ceremony.

My cock auto reacts to her enticing form; she's fucking beautiful.

"Into the bed," I command, gently but sternly.

She does as I say again.

Good Girl.

What I do next has even me questioning my own sanity.

I walk over, take the cover, and pull them up over her. She looks at me a little puzzled.

"You're not going to join me?"

"Not tonight, Angel; you need actual sleep."

I lean over and kiss her forehead softly.

Her honey eyes look at me, almost pleading for me to change my mind.

I have to walk away before I do something I know I shouldn't.

I have almost reached the door when she calls out for me.

"Adrian, please stay."

I turn to look at her; she's sitting up in the bed, holding the blanket to her.

"Just for a little while?" she hesitates. "You did promise your brother you'd look after me."

Then she offers me a wicked little grin. Shaking my head, I walk back toward her.

"Okay, Angel." I climb in the bed next to her, fully clothed, pulling her into my chest, and I lay there cuddling with her as she settles in.

"Get some rest," I say softly and kiss the top of her head.

Once her breathing calms, and her chest rises and falls in a soft rhythm, and I know she's asleep, I slowly peel away from her, climbing out of the bed. Having to adjust myself in my pants as I stand, I've been hard all night and wanting to be buried deep inside her.

Why was I leaving again? I question myself.

I found a piece of paper and scribbled a note on it for her, setting it next to her phone, then doing the unexplainable, I leave.

* * *

I spent the rest of the night after leaving Emmy restless, not being able to shut down my own mind. I had only managed a few hours of light sleep before giving up and getting out of bed.

I don't know what I'm going to do about the Emmy situation yet, but what I want to do is head over there right now. I didn't want to leave last night.

She wasn't supposed to get under my skin the way she did. I had barely known the girl for two days, and I already couldn't stop thinking about her. My cock reacts to even thoughts of her. I am like a walking hard on.

When really I shouldn't even be entertaining the idea of her and I, Ryan would fucking kill me.

I don't know if I am capable of being in a relationship with someone, let alone what my brother would say about it. I don't even want to think about what that conversation would look like.

Yet here I was not being able to wipe her out of my thoughts while also fighting with emotions regarding Sarah—emotions I had done a good job of keeping pushed under the rug until now.

After Emmy had told me what Tonya had said, I couldn't get what happened to Sarah out of my mind. So,

I figured it might be time for more answers. I know that I will never fully be available to anyone if I can't move forward from what happened to Sarah, move forward from the guilt and uncertainty of it all.

They say time heals all, but I have yet to do any healing.

If I want a chance in hell of even trying with Emmy, I know that I need to close out my Sarah chapters. I needed to get the answers I have been avoiding for twelve years.

I've spent a long time wondering what I had done to make her act like that.

Now I was suspicious Tonya might have played a role in her walking away from me. How could she live with herself?

Rubbing my temples, I push back from my laptop. I had spent most of the morning going back through old phone records and text messages between Sarah and I trying to find a clue as to when things started to shift.

I can see now that a few weeks before the wedding, she had started to pull back, acting a little different. I hadn't noticed it then, or I wrote it off as nerves.

I was going to need Anthony's help if I wanted to decipher all this.

He wasn't just a bartender for me; he was one of my closest friends. I met him in Oregon some years back. He was a little younger than me, had found himself in some trouble, and needed a fresh start. I had felt a responsibility to help him out. Ryan was already living here in Utah. I already owned this home here, so it seemed like a good spot to send Anthony to make a new start.

With a little startup help from Ryan, I opened Tipsy Roots Bar and Grill and had Anthony take over managing it when he was old enough.

Anthony was a wiz with electronics; he could easily have taken up a job working with Ryan in the tech field, but since he's had a felony and didn't go to school, not many places would even give him a shot. That's not the case with Ryan, though; he didn't care about any of that and would have given him a job at Cresting; it was Anthony that didn't want it; he always says he's more comfortable where he is, staying under the radar.

Grabbing my phone, I sent off a text to him.

Me: I need your help with something.
Anthony: What's up boss?
Me: Was hoping you could work some magic on an out-of-date phone for me.
Anthony: I can try.
Me: Great, I'll swing it by the bar in a bit.

I don't have to ask if he will be there; his apartment is above the bar.

Walking around my living room, I wondered why I ever kept this house; it felt so empty and too big. I didn't stay here much anyway; most of the time it was empty. When I bought the place, I had intended to spend more time here to be closer to my brother, but after Sarah's accident, I distanced myself from everything. I stayed in Oregon more and more, rarely coming back to Utah.

It's not that Sarah and I lived here because we didn't; we never got the chance to share this house like I had intended.

Still, I can't help the guilty feeling forming in the pit of my stomach when I think about bringing Emmy here. I have never brought a hook up here before, because even if we didn't get the life we had planned, this house was supposed to be for Sarah and I.

Every choice I have made since first seeing Emmy walking into my bar has been out of character for me.

Walking out of the room, I head down the hall and into the oversized closet attached to my room.

Grabbing down a worn brown box I had shoved up here and tried to forget about.

The box was full of memories, I tried to forget most days, old pictures, momentums from our short time together, and a clear bag labeled evidence.

It had the items collected from Sarah's car in it. I have never opened the bag. After the cops closed and ruled her wreck an accident, they gave me the bag, and I shoved it into this stupid old box with the rest of our memories.

Pulling open the bag, the pain in my chest gets stronger. My heart pounding with the pain from that day, and floods of memories rise back to the surface.

Hurrying, I grab the one item I was looking for and close it back up. Shoving those memories back down before they consumed me completely.

The little phone in my hand feels heavier than it should. I can see her talking on it, how her little hand played with the ring attached to the back of the purple case, and see her laughing while on the phone with her mom or a friend. I can picture her bright eyes light up and that contagious smile filling her face.

The pain pounds in my chest again, and I wonder why the hell I'm putting myself through this again. Clearly, I still needed to work through some shit.

Stuffing the phone in my pocket, I head out of the house.

* * *

Anthony is waiting in the parking lot of the bar when I pull in. Not sure why he's out here, but I'm not going to question it; it's not important to me.

Getting out of the car, I walk over to him. The gravel crunches under my feet. I look down, seeing there is still blood stained on the ground beneath my feet from the other night.

Shaking my head to clear the images of the guy holding Emmy down on the hood of her car out of my mind. One fucking issue at a time, or I'm going to give myself a fucking aneurysm.

First, I need to get answers on Sarah, and then I can decide what the hell I'm going to do with the Emmy situation.

"I haven't tried to turn it on; I don't think the battery is even good anymore," I say walking to Anthony.

"No problem, boss. I will do what I can."

"I'm interested in what's on it."

Anthony takes the phone from me. "I'll save anything I can off it." He lets out a sigh, and then adds, "You sure you really want to do this? It's not going to bring her back."

"I need to do this." I sound more confident than I actually feel about it.

Looking at the old phone and turning it over in his hands a few times, he looks back at me.

"Okay, give me a few hours, and I'll let you know if anything is savable."

"Thanks, man. I owe ya one."

"Anything else you need?" he asks.

"Just let me know if you can restore anything."

"Will do, boss," he says before walking back toward the bar.

A few hours and I will hopefully have some answers. I don't know what I'm actually expecting he will find, I think there should be some messages or something from Tonya on there, maybe they will have answers as to why she left.

I tell myself again that digging in the past is what will make it so I can move on.

All I really know is that I want answers.

With that part in motion, I'm left with the next task on my agenda: I needed to check on Emmy.

Getting back to my car, I open the door and slide onto the leather seats. As I head out of the parking lot, I wonder how different my life might have been if Sarah had survived, if we had gotten married. Would we have had kids? Would we still be together now? A million other what-if's fill my mind.

Halfway to Emmy's place, my phone pings. A text message comes across the screen in the car. I give the voice command for the car to read it out loud.

Message from Tonya: *Sorry if I was out of line last night; I must have had a little too much to drink. I'm so embarrassed. Let me make it up to you.*

She didn't deserve a response in my book. I have no doubt she knew exactly what she was doing. I have no idea where she ever got the idea I would be with her in any way, even before Sarah. I had known she was interested, but at no point did I ever entertain that fantasy of hers.

Pulling up to Emmy's apartment complex, I was glad to see her car was still in its designated stall.

I had meant to come back this morning, but my mind had been stuck on Sarah, and my obsession for more answers was overriding my logical thoughts, not that I was sure any of my recent thoughts were all that logical.

I'm not even sure that Emmy is anything more than an intense sexual attraction, but I know either way, this is not fair to her. I don't know that I'll ever be mentally available for someone like I was for Sarah.

I'm just hoping that maybe I can get some closure now; it's been too long that I have been holding onto all this hurt. I have let what happened and not knowing what truly went wrong define me for so many years.

It's why I used girls the way I do now, why I only let it be sexual and nothing more, never more. If I didn't get close to someone, they couldn't get hurt, and I couldn't get hurt.

I had no plans of changing that either. I was fine that way, that's what I have always told myself anyway.

I didn't want the responsibility of someone's life on my hands ever again. I didn't want that guilt when something went wrong.

Love 'em and leave 'em was my way, and not love in the feelings type of way; nope, only the physical bang out. It's just the way it was—well until now.

Until her.

She makes me want things again, want a relationship, want the life I've missed out on, and want to be needed by someone more than just the physical.

I need to get my mind straight. Because this chick is messing with all the feelings.

Emmy

When I woke, I found Adrian was already gone. A note was left saying he would come by sometime this morning and check in on me.

I was both sad and excited. I had fallen asleep in his arms last night; I couldn't remember the last time I had slept so well. It was perfect.

However, after hours had passed with no word from him, I'd resolved into thinking Adrian wasn't going to show today.

I had made a fool out of myself last night; I practically begged for him to stay with me. I had wanted more than just to fall asleep in his arms, but he had declined. That should have been a sign. What was I thinking? That is not how you have a one-night stand. Opening the notes section on my phone again, I added another line: things I need to remember if I want to try the whole one-night stand thing again, because, so far, I failed at it.

How to have a one-night stand
Never go home with a stranger from the bar
Never develop feelings for the guy
Never, ever invite him to stay over a second night

I changed into comfy clothes that I don't mind getting paint on, an oversized t-shirt, and shorts that were so short they showed part of my ass.

Sitting cross-legged on the floor in front of the coffee table, a canvas, and some paints spread all around me.

It was afternoon now, and I still hadn't heard from him at all. Him not reaching out to me at all hurt more than I liked to admit.

He wasn't anyone to me, so why did I care so much?

It was another reminder that I was being stupid in this situation that I had the right idea before when I was going to leave and forget about him all together.

He was just like every other guy that had been in my life; I was an inconvenience, and he didn't want me.

When he came to my house last night, it had gotten me confused all over again. Why did he have to be Ryan's brother? Why couldn't I have just had a normal, meaningless hookup? Why did I care that he wasn't reaching out to me?

Why bother tracking me down last night, only to leave again?

I needed to get stuff out of my mind. So, I was doing what I always did when I needed to work through shit. I was laying paint to the canvas and letting whatever came to mind flow through the paintbrush. This is something I have been doing for a long time to help ease the overactive emotions that run through my mind.

* * *

Looking down on my painting; seeing an image that wasn't my typical subject matter. It had just been on my mind all night, and I needed to release it in some way or another, and since it seemed like I wasn't going to get the relief in the way I had been dreaming about, this would have to do.

The painting was almost complete; it featured a lady kneeling, her butt touching the top of her heels, her toes curled forward, pressing against a mattress, her back arched with her arms pulled back, intricately woven with rope wrapped around them, in a shibari-like fashion, with a beautiful knotted design from bicep to wrists, where her hands cross and rest against her ass. Her hair pulled back in a loose braid, and she was looking over her shoulder so you could see the side profile of her face, and the desire and need reflecting in her eyes.

After adding the finishing touches, I was finally happy with how it turned out. It's beautiful, sensual, and a real expression of art in so many ways.

It wasn't until its completion that I noticed I had subconsciously modeled the girl in the painting after myself.

It hadn't been done intentionally; however, there was no mistaking the striking resemblance.

Knock. Knock.

The sound from the door makes me jump, smacking my knee on the coffee table. Spilling the cup of dirty brush cleaning water.

"Shit."

Thank goodness it was on the floor and not on the painting.

Knock. Knock. Knock.

The sound even louder this time.

"Just a minute," I call out

Scrambling to get to my feet and find something to soak up the paint water, this is going to screw up the carpet so bad.

"Emmy, let me in." Adrian bellows from the other side of the door.

"Give me a minute," I yell back.

Grabbing a towel and the dish soap from the kitchen, I try to scrub some of the paint water up.

"EMMY!" His voice was loud.

I couldn't quite tell if he was angry or worried. I stop my pursuit to clean up. Stomping to the door, flinging it open,

Adrian stops mid-swing to knock again.

"Calm down, ya big brute," I say, annoyed. "You're going to get the police called."

He looks past me, scanning the room, before dropping his hand and looking me over.

"You okay?" He huffs.

"Of course, I'm okay."

I pull him inside and close the door behind him.

"What is all over you?" he asks now, really looking at me.

"Paint. Why wouldn't I be okay?" I look up at him, hands on my hips.

Adrian looks at me again with skepticism in his eyes.

"*Uh*, I heard noises, and you screamed." He shrugs, looking around the small space.

Exasperated, I toss my hands in the air, in a whatever indication, walking back to the mess I left, bending down, and beginning to scrub up more of the dirty liquid. Now I'm more irritated with him than I was this morning.

"Yeah, some jerk scared me, and I hit my knee on the table, causing a disastrous mess."

Following me into the living room, he looks around again, still searching for something out of the ordinary, I guess.

"I didn't mean to scare you." He looks at me sheepishly.

"Yeah, well, I wasn't expecting you, and I was kind of in my own world."

"I told you I was going to come over today." Adrian looks down, noticing the painting, reaching down to pick up the canvas.

"Be careful. It's not fully dry."

Getting back on my feet, I take the towel and rinse it out in the sink, running the water over it until the paint comes out.

Glancing back toward Adrian as he analyzes the picture.

"Yeah, well, the day is more than half over, so."

I ring and re-dampen the towel, walking back over to the smaller paint smeared spot on the carpet, and pressing the damp towel into the spot. I know it's not going to take it out, and I'm probably going to have to pay to have it professionally cleaned.

"There goes my security deposit," I mumble to myself.

Abandoning my efforts, I toss the towel down on the coffee table and take a seat on the couch.

Adrian is still examining my work. Watching him look over the painting makes me nervous.

I don't usually show off my work like this and never something so personally vulnerable.

After what seems like forever. He looks at me.

"You did this?"

"I did."

"It's amazing. I love the soft tones and the low light, the slight reddening. You can picture the ropes leaving on her soft skin and how you captured her desire in it. Truly, it's beautiful."

He says with admiration, which I wasn't expecting.

"Thanks."

"Sorry about scaring you."

Adrian sets the painting back down on the table, taking a seat next to me on the couch.

I shift shyly next to him, hating how my breathing changes the second he's close to me.

"Is that something you have done before?" Adrian asks, intrigued, pointing to the painting.

"Nope." I look away nervously, wondering if he notices the resemblances.

He grabs my chin, turning my face to his, and I close my eyes. His close presence, his touch does things to me.

I hate that I feel so out of control when he's near, like all rational thought leaves my brain.

"Look at me," he commands. "Don't shy away from me."

I open my eyes slowly and am met with his steely gaze locking with mine.

"You don't have to hide from me, Emmy..." He practically growls at me.

"I'm not hiding." I snap back.

Pulling back from his hand, still grasping my face. A look crosses his face briefly; he seems torn.

"Is it something you want to try?" His tone was smooth again, no hit of the dominance from a moment ago.

"I don't know much about it; I only began to look into it more this morning."

"Ever since you tied me up the other night, it's been something that appealed to me," I answer honestly.

He gives me a small smile. "I like that you're looking into things that you might like."

My skin heats; please don't let him notice the flush of color. I internally beg. He makes me nervous, and my body aches for his touch all at the same time.

Trying to change the topic before I let my body rule over. There are things Adrian and I should most definitely talk about that don't include me being tied up at his mercy.

"What took you so long today?"

That torn look again, he shifts uncomfortably, adding distance between us, running his hand through his hair.

"I had a lot on my mind this morning."

His vague answer only brings back my earlier irritation. I don't know why I react to him like this; it's like he flipped a switch in me; my sexual desire and every other emotion gets out of whack with him.

"I don't think this is a good idea," I say, motioning back and forth between the two of us.

"So, you don't want me to do this with you?" Pointing again to my painting, he leans in closer. I can smell his fresh, intoxicating scent, and just like it has before, it makes me want him to do anything and everything he wants to me.

"No, no, I don't." I breathe out, not even believing my own words.

His arms come around me, and his body leans into me. I press back into the corner of the couch.

His lips trail along my neck.

"You sure about that?" he whispers into my ear. His lips brushing along it lightly.

It sends shivers through me.

"To let someone do that to you would be to give them total control over your body; are you sure you don't want me to have that?"

My head tilts back, and a low moan escapes my lips. His body is so close to mine, I'm sure he can feel the heat coming from me.

His lips find the soft skin of my neck again, he kisses down from the base below my ear to my collarbone.

All convictions I had about us earlier are thrown out the window as my body melts under him.

"Look at me, Angel."

I do as he asks, meeting his gaze for the second time today.

"Now tell me you don't want me to do this," he says, almost begging me to tell him to stop as he leans his head down again, capturing my mouth with his.

I want to resist, but I can't. I open up to his tongue along my lips.

Kissing him back with the need I've felt all night. I reach up and grab around his neck, pulling him to deepen the kiss.

So much for talking; I was a goner. There was no way I was going to stop him.

Adrian

This is not what I had planned when I came over here; this was all kinds of fucked up.

Initially, I was worried she was in trouble, or worse, she had someone in her place with her.

Here, I was still completely fucked up over Sarah, yet I was jealous at the mere thought of her having someone else here. The thought of someone else touching her drove me mad. I had no right to claim her as mine, but damned if I didn't want to.

Then when I walked in, seeing her in that grungy shirt that was at least a size or two too big for her and then there was her painting.

The desire she portrayed in it. It made me want to do all kinds of naughty things to her. Binding her wrist the other night was one thing, tying someone up like that was a whole other level of intimacy.

I asked her if she wanted me to stop. I needed her to be the one to stop me because I couldn't stop myself. But she didn't, she didn't stop me; she wanted all of this as much as I did, her body responding to mine just like it had that first night.

She shifts under me, and I press closer, her legs wrap around my waist, my cock hard, pressing against my jeans. I know she can feel it pressed against her pussy.

I'm rewarded with her heels digging into my ass and pulling me even closer. We are as close together as two people could be, with the thin layer of our clothes being the only thing separating us.

The couch is almost too narrow for the both of us to be lying on it in this way.

I press her into the cushions. I need to be deep inside her, so deep I won't know where I begin and she ends, and I need her like she is the answer to all my problems.

The buzzing and vibration in my pocket make me pull back; reality has a way of rearing its ugly head.

She drops her legs, and with a hurt look in her eyes, guts me as I push away from her and off the couch.

Standing, taking the phone out of my pocket. Anthony's name flashes across the screen, and just as a bucket of cold water would have felt, I instantly chill.

"Sorry, I need to get this."

"Hey, man, what's up?" I answer as calmly as possible. Stepping away from Emmy, leaving her alone on the couch, I walk into the small attached kitchen.

"I'm sending you a file; I just wanted to give you a heads up."

"So, you were able to get something, then?"

Guilt working its way through me as I glance over at Emmy, who is now picking up her paint supplies and straightening her living space.

"You're sure you want me to send it to you?"

I can hear the concern in his voice. It takes me a second to reply, as I question why this is so important to me.

"I'm sure. Just send over the files."

I have blamed myself for so much related to Sarah's death. I need some answers that's what finally wins out and rules my decision. I need to know what I did wrong.

"Got it, boss," he then adds, "if you need to talk, I'll be at the bar all night."

With no further explanation, he hangs up.

Leaning against the counter, I wait for the message to come through. Drifting back to my thoughts from earlier, picturing what life would be like with Sarah, what we would be doing now? Would her body react to my touch in the same way Emmy's does? I try to remember how it was the few times we were together. Would she be so willing to let me explore with her? Would she give herself fully to me, trusting me with her pleasure the way Emmy does?

Fuck, I run my hand through my hair.

I glance at the blank screen, wondering if he changed his mind and isn't going to send it to me.

Emmy walks into the kitchen, rubbing my arm.

"Everything all right?"

I look at her, and the look on my face must show the anger I'm currently feeling as she drops her hand and takes a small step backward.

"Fine, just dealing with some old shit."

She turns to deposit the rag and cup into the sink, and I feel the coldness settling between us. She's only inches away, and all I want to do is grab her around the waist and pull her against me.

Reaching out to her, intent on doing just that, when my phone buzzes in my hand, ending the moment once more.

Emmy looks over her shoulder at me, pain in her eyes.

"I'm sorry." Not knowing exactly what I'm apologizing for, this interruption, or everything since I met her.

Giving me a small smile, she turns back to the sink. I'm pretty sure she's just trying to keep herself busy. I don't know what to say to her, and I don't think she knows what to say to me.

Pulling up the email, I notice there are three main attachments.

'Photos, Text, and Deleted.' I read over his email; he was able to recover a lot of stuff but not everything; most of the stuff is only from the week leading up to the accident.

Taking in a deep breath, I click on the file.

Seeing her photos again nearly breaks me. There are photos of us, selfies she would force me to take, photos of Tonya, her, Ryan, and myself when we used to all hang out. I scroll through only a few pictures before closing that file; its too much to see. It may have been over a decade ago, but not to me; it's just as fresh in my mind as if it all happened only yesterday.

I skip the text file for now and decide to dive into what she would have deleted. Deleted calendar events, deleted messages, and other files fill my screen as I scroll through the first few.

It's like slow motion as I watch my phone drop to the ground, slumping against the counter.

The sudden pounding in my ears is so loud. Emmy, in front of me in an instant; her lips are moving, but I can't hear what she is saying over the pounding. Where is that coming from.

I look around trying to understand what's going on, and when I realize the noise pounding is me, the heavy beat of my heart pumping blood wildly, with the pressure, I wonder how it hasn't beat right out of my chest.

I scarcely register Emmy's small hands trying to hold me up.

Fear etched across her face.

I grip my chest and try to breathe.

"Adrian." My name comes out of her mouth, but sounds like she's in a fishbowl. Her grip on me slips as I slip further down to the cabinet until I'm seated on the floor.

Emmy crouches down next to me, pulling out her own phone.

Her words barely register as she says she's calling an ambulance.

An ambulance—why would she call an ambulance?

"No." I manage to choke out, grabbing her wrist.

She stops typing on her phone. Looking at me, I can see unshed tears glistening in her eyes.

"No ambulance." I don't even recognize the quivering voice coming out of my mouth.

She wraps her arms around my neck. "Are you okay?" she asks shakily.

I breathe in her soft and creamy scent and steady myself more; she smells like wild flowers. I pull her down to me, so she is sitting on my lap.

The pounding easing in my chest.

I don't know how long I hold her—seconds, minutes, hours… She doesn't say anything as I hold her to me, taking in rhythmic breaths. Her body was still shaking silently, or was it my body shaking? I'm not entirely sure.

"I'm okay," I finally say.

She releases her hold on me, sitting up straight but she doesn't make a move to leave my lap.

"What's happened?"

That's when I remember my abandoned phone.

"It's Sarah." The deep pain in my voice

Emmy looks at me, confused. "What's Sarah?"

"I'm so sorry, Angel," I say, rubbing my hand up and down her back.

"I don't understand?"

Pushing off the ground, I stand, pulling her up with me. I don't release her fully, not wanting to lose the contact I have left.

I kiss her cheek. Needing her more than I care to admit. This is so fucked; I know in this moment I'm using her, just like I've used the women before her.

I'm using her now to erase the pain of Sarah, but unlike the others before her, she makes the pain go away when I'm with her; none of the women before her made the ache go away like she does.

Not knowing where to even start to explain, not knowing if what was on the phone can even be trusted… Of course, it can; why else would she have deleted them? She should have come to me; she should have told me.

Fuck.

"I had Anthony restore some content on Sarah's old phone. After what Tonya said to you the other night, it had me wondering if she had said something to Sarah to scare her off; she had tried to get me to sleep with her before the wedding, and I had thought maybe she said something." I pause, reliving the pain of that day.

"This whole time I've blamed myself; I have spent the last twelve years wondering what I could have done to make her run from me, from us, from the life we talked about having together. I was sure I did something to fuck it all up."

"You can't change the past, Adrian. The accident wasn't your fault."

"I never saw it like that, Emmy. We were getting married; she ran from me, and that's the last I saw her alive."

I run my hand through my hair.

"Did you get answers, Adrian? Do you feel better now? Cuz from where I'm standing, I thought you were going to die just now. I thought you were having a heart attack, and I was going to lose you." Her voice is full of emotion, pain, and fear, evident in her words.

She takes a step back, away from me. "Why would you want to relive it?"

"You don't understand." My tone comes out harsher than I meant it to be.

"You're right, Adrian. I don't. I don't get it at all. I understood when you told me what happened, how fucked up it was; I even understand why you do the whole one-night stand thing and don't get in relationships. But I don't understand why you're still letting it control ALL of you."

"You sound like a jealous child right now," I chide

"How can I be jealous of someone who isn't even here, Adrian?" Her voice lowers; she sounds defeated; it doesn't hold that fire from a moment ago.

I reach for her, but she pulls back.

"I hope it was worth it, Adrian."

"Emmy, please understand that I have lived with the thoughts that I did something wrong, that I was responsible and cost the life of the woman I loved, who I thought loved me, who I was going to have a family with."

"I do understand."

Picking up my phone, I glance back at the deleted files, text, pictures, and Dr. appointments I never knew about.

I hate that Emmy is right; I hate that I gave up the past twelve years of my life because of a guilt that wasn't even mine to carry.

I think that's what makes this so much harder now. I had this image of Sarah always in my mind.

Even still right now, I know that had she told me, I would have forgiven her. I would have stayed with her; I would have fought for her.

This blame I have carried for so long wasn't mine, though. All this time, I thought I had done something, but she had; she betrayed me, and I don't know how to process it.

"Was it worth it?" Emmy asks.

I don't know how to answer. I know she is asking if digging it back up was worth it, were the answers I got worth it the pain, and if continuing to relive it was worth it.

Maybe she's right. I shouldn't have gone digging in the first place. I should have mourned and moved forward with life in the first place, like normal people do; at least then I would have had the good times to think about still. Now, it's all tainted.

"She was cheating."

I hated even saying the words. I hated the bile that rose in my throat.

"I'm sorry she did that to you." Emmy is standing a few feet away from me, holding herself protectively. I want to tell her how I need to just hold her and how she can make the hurt, the pain go away, even if it's only for a little bit.

"She was pregnant. I don't know if it was mine or..." I trail off.

Emmy's eyes soften as she looks at me, I can tell she's holding back tears.

"I am sorry, Adrian."

I reach for her, but this time she doesn't pull away; she lets me wrap my arm around her waist. She's stiff as I hold her, something changed between us, and I'm not exactly sure what to do about it.

"I can't fix it, Adrian; no matter what I do, I can't make everything all better for you. You have to do that on your own, and I can't be the one left here alone and broken when you finally feel whole again."

There it is, as if she has heard my internal thoughts, she's right too. I want to tell her that it's not like that and that it will be fine as long as I'm with her, but I don't know if that's even possible. I don't know if I can ever be what she deserves.

"Just one night," I whisper into her hair as I hold her to me.

She grabs my upper arms and holds me tight. Leaning her head back, I look into her honey brown eyes, and the pain I feel reflected back to me in them. Tears are slipping from them, rolling in a little trail down her beautiful cheeks.

"That's all it was supposed to be," she replies.

I kiss the tears away, following the trail down her face, until I reach the corner of her mouth, capturing her lips hard, and kissing her with all the pain I carry.

A whimper escapes past her lips. I can't leave it like this; I need her.

Pulling back, breaking our kiss, and breathing heavily. I grip her waist, picking her up and setting her on the counter. She squeals as I do.

"Please. Emmy, please," I beg her. I know it's not fair of me to ask, "One more time?" I'm an asshole for not just leaving, but I fucking need her right now. I need to not feel anything but her right now. I am doing exactly what she said I would do; use her to feel better.

A feral primal need—a possessive need to be inside her—overtakes all other thoughts.

Emmy

Breathing heavily, I adjust on the counter top as Adrian slips my shorts down and off of me, tossing them aside.

I should have said no; even now I should stop him, but I don't want to. As much as it's going to hurt me when he walks out that door, I need him now.

The anguish mars his beautiful features; his eyes are filled with sadness and feral need.

I didn't know anything could exist that was as intense as the chemistry I have with Adrian. I'm like a moth drawn to the flame, flying so close I can feel the fire beginning to consume me.

I know he's not good for me, but I still want that warmth of his touch. I need the fire that burns across my skin as his fingers trail my body.

He was right about something earlier. I was jealous, not of Sarah but of what she took with her when she left him; she took his hope for a future.

I can't give that back to him; he has to find it on his own, and I'm not strong enough to fight this battle. He's not mine to keep; he never was.

But I can give him this; right here right now, I can give him me.

His hands caress up my sides, pulling my shirt up as he goes. I lift my arms over my head as he strips it, freeing me from it.

Exposing me to him.

I propped on my elbows, holding myself up.

"Spread wider for me, Angel."

I do, letting my knees fall wider, and scooting so the edge of my ass is on the edge of the counter, the arches of my feet pressed on the edge of the counter for support.

I watch as Adrian undoes his belt, dropping his pants to the ground, his stiff cock pressing against the thin fabric of his boxers.

My chest rising and falling with each heavy breath.

He takes a moment to look me over as he rids himself of his remaining clothes.

"So fucking beautiful," he says while stroking up and down his long length.

Stepping between my legs, Adrian positions himself. Grabbing my hips, he pulls me to him, slamming deep inside of me in one swift movement.

I let out a scream as he filled me so tight, pushing and stretching me. He groans as he pulls himself almost completely out of me, only to slam back in. His eyes are wild, like he's somewhere else completely, and my arms are weak. I feel like they won't hold me as he takes what he needs from me.

My head lulls back, closing my eyes as his grip on me gets harder. His mouth finds my nipples, taking each in turn sucking and nipping at them until they are hard peaks. I arch up into him.

"Lift your legs over my shoulder," he commands.

I do as he asks; the shift in position allows me to lay my back flat against the countertop.

He takes from me greedily, pumping in and out in long, hard motions.

Everything about this is different from the first time I was with him. The first time we were together, it had been all about my pleasure; this is solely about his need. Nothing about this time is soft and caring; it's hard and fast.

Yet I still felt like a goddess being worshiped. All of my nerves are on fire, feeling everything he was taking. He was leaving a trail of fire as he kissed along my thighs that rested on his shoulders.

Adrian thrusts harder and harder, taking one of his hands from my waist. He slides it between us, finding my clit, pressing, and rubbing as he pounds me.

The pleasure builds inside of me; I can feel myself tighten around him as he brings me to climax.

Even in this frenzied fuck, he brings me to orgasm.

His breathing is heavy, and sweat drips down his chest. He groans in pleasure as I ride out my climax, pulling him over the edge with me.

I push myself up on my forearms. Slowly, he slips out of me, gently releasing my legs from his shoulders, and letting them drape over the edge of the counter.

I feel empty in more ways than one as our connection is severed.

Turning around in the small kitchen, he grabs a clean washcloth from a stack next to the sink, wetting it. Coming back to wipe away the evidence of his own release from me.

He helps me off the counter, then cleans himself up. Not saying anything as we both get dressed.

I stand awkwardly in my own kitchen, not knowing what to say or do.

What I want to do is just hold him, I want to feel his arms around me again. It's ridiculous, and I sound like a crazy person. I have only known him all of three days. These feelings are too much.

"I'm sorry," he finally says, breaking the silence.

"Me too," I say, and I walk to him, standing on tiptoe. I kiss him on the cheek.

He grabs my hand, holding it for a minute. I can see he's war-ing with himself, the expressions on his face changing.

"My Angel." He chokes out. Bringing my hand to his lips, kissing the back of it. Letting it go, he turns and heads to the door.

I can't do anything but stand there and watch him walk away.

I know it's for the best, but I can't help the sinking feeling in my chest or stop the tears that leak down my face. An emptiness I wasn't expecting takes over me. It feels like the world is on fire around me, and all I can do is watch it burn.

I never dreamed I would feel like this. I didn't want to fall in love with him; I don't even know how it's possible, but I did. It has all been so fast, and now I've lost him without ever really even having him in the first place.

"Well, this is going to make family dinner awkward." I laugh and cry in the open room, trying to find the humor in it all.

* * *

All night I had hoped he would call me, text me, anything, but he never did. I spent most of the night scrubbing the kitchen, not knowing what else to do with my time.

After a quick shower, I threw on a tank and jean shorts, I made myself some coffee, and grabbed my phone, once again pulling open the notepad.

How to have a one-night stand
Never go home with a stranger from the bar
Never develop feelings for the guy
Never invite him to stay over a second night
Never ever have sex with him a second time

I really want to talk to Lucy, but I know she won't have her cell on her, and I am not about to call her parents landline, so I decided to send a text off to my mom.

Me: Hey, Mom, I hope you are having an amazing time on your honeymoon. Love you.

I don't really expect a text back, and I feel a little guilty that I don't even know where they went, so I don't know what time of day it is or anything.

The painting is still sitting on the coffee table; it causes a pain in my chest to look at it.

I no longer want it; I also don't want to throw it away. I truly love how it turned out. Deciding to list it online in an attempt to get some money out of it and sell it to someone who doesn't know me or what it meant to me.

I'm angry with Adrian for not letting go of the past, for not wanting to live for a future, and for not being what either of us needs.

How can I be so angry with him? In reality, I don't even know him. And how can I be mad at someone for doing the same thing I have been doing? I have been so afraid of what the future could bring that I haven't made any plans for myself since finishing school. I've been holding myself back, afraid that I could fail, afraid that after I spent all this time being what I thought others needed or wanted me to be that I didn't truly know how to be me.

Meeting Adrian pushed my boundaries in so many ways; it has opened my eyes to a part of my sexuality I didn't know I craved, and it's made me feel alive.

After spending all night feeling sorry for myself, I've decided I'm going to try to do something positive instead of letting myself get wrapped up in the situation, and what could be if things went different?

It would be so easy to let the depression and fear seep in and consume me, but I won't let it, I have worked so hard mentally to let this influence my self-worth.

So, I'm going to take that energy Adrian ignited and take a chance on my own life. I know changing my situation is the only way I'm going to move past all of this.

Determined to make this work, I pull out my laptop and pull up an art auction site. It only takes me a few minutes to create an account and upload my piece.

After the painting is listed, I switch my search to something else I have put off, not thinking I could do it.

I look up flights to Italy. Lucy and I had talked about it when she first got accepted into culinary school. She had tried to convince me to go bringing up how I could go explore the history and the art.

I have just been too scared to step out of my comfort zone. I'm now glad that I at least went with her to get our passports when she first applied to the school out of the country. I hadn't actually thought I would use it, but wanted to have it just in case.

Besides, what better way to get some space from my current situation and push my own boundaries?

There's no way I could afford to go the whole time Lucy will be there. She is going to one of the finest culinary schools to learn everything about all different cuisines and to get a degree in hospitality and business management, so she will be there for a couple years. But if this painting sells and I list a few others I have done, I should be able to scrape together enough funds for a few weeks at least. And I could always list my car now that I have a new one clean and clear.

Ping

I am surprised when my phone notification goes off next to me.

Mom: Having the time of my life, Belize is beautiful. Hope you're feeling better

Me: I'm feeling much better. I am glad you are having a good time.

Mom: Love you; see you in a week sweetheart

Me: Can't wait to hear all about Belize. I have things I want to share with you too

Mom: Stay safe

Me: You too, Mom, tell Ryan, I said hi

I smile for the first time since Adrian walked out, and I really am glad she has Ryan. She seems truly happy with him, and their dogs get along, so that's a bonus. I laugh.

They even hired a professional just to doggy-sit. Like I couldn't have gone and checked on the mongrels.

Having a plan to fund the trip, booking flights, and talking with my mom has me feeling a little more optimistic than yesterday.

This will be good for me; I just know it.

When Lucy gets home, I have to run the idea by her, hoping she will let me stay with her. It's not like we haven't talked about it before; I had been apprehensive then, but even if staying with her doesn't work out, I'll just find a place on my own.

I need as much space between Adrian and myself as possible to move forward, because even now I want to call him, want to make sure he's okay, I want to be wrapped in his arms, to feel that spark that always runs along my skin when he's near.

I even want to tell him about Italy and how excited I am to explore the art there.

He's the type of man I could get completely consumed by; the fire has already scorched my skin. I know that if I let him, I could be completely engulfed and burnt to ashes by that man.

I just can't do that to myself; I can't let that happen; I won't pine over something I can't change; I won't do what he has been doing for the past twelve years.

After all, we were just a chance encounter at a bar; we were never truly meant to be.

Adrian

I spent the rest of that day in self-pity and regret. The first week away from her, if I'm being honest with myself. I thought I saw Emmy everywhere, even at the bar. I was in the back office, and I could have sworn she walked into the bar on the security system, her golden hair flowing down her back, but it wasn't her. I had run out of the office so fast I nearly scared the poor girl to death. After that, I knew I had to take the steps to fix myself.

I have picked up the phone to call Emmy almost every day since I walked out of her apartment over two weeks ago.

I just couldn't do it, not while I still needed to straighten my life out. It wouldn't be fair to put her through this, not after leaving the way I did.

The first step I took to letting go of the past was to list my house in Entrada. Even though I never lived in it with Sarah, it's a reminder of what it was supposed to be, and I was getting to a place of letting all that go.

Luckily for me, the house sold quickly, and was only on the market a couple days.

I had spent a little more time going through the files Anthony had sent over; the more I dug, the more I found she had hidden from me, so much I wish I would have known years ago. All these years, I have felt like I did something to make her walk away, that there was something different I could have done that would have changed everything. But that guilt was misplaced; I didn't hide from Sarah; she hid from me; she had a whole separate life I wasn't a part of; she lied to me.

And as much as it hurts, I can't fix who I've been the past twelve years because of it or change all that I have lost out on because of what happened, and at this point I don't want to anyway.

Everything I went through, every choice I made shaped who I am now. Of course, there are parts I wish I could change, things I've done that I am not proud of, but I have to believe that fate had its hand in leading me to where I am and showing me the man I want to be going forward.

One thing I was sure of now is that I'm not going to deny what I felt for Emmy; it was real. No matter how fast it had gotten to that or how it started, I wanted to be with her.

I needed her to be in my life.

I knew that if I had any chance of winning her back, I had to show her I was making changes that I could do the work for me.

The day after I left Emmy standing in her apartment, I went to see a therapist. I was getting help to let go of the guilt and anger.

Yet with all the work I've been putting in these past couple weeks, I know the hardest part is going to be coming clean to Ryan and Joanne. And showing Emmy that she's worth it to all to me, she makes it all worth it.

The vibration of my phone brings me back to the present.

As if he was reading my mind a text came across my phone from Ryan.

Ryan: You free tonight?
Me: Yeah, what's up?
Ryan: Just doing a little dinner and would like you to be here, haven't seen you since the wedding.
Me: Sounds good; what time?
Ryan: Six-thirty
Me: I'll be there

Well, I guess now is as good a time as any. I don't want to blind side Emmy, though, so I decide to send her a text.

Me: Can we talk?

After a long time without a reply, I decided to send off another one.

Me: Emmy, please; I need to talk to you.

After another hour, she still hadn't replied. Did she think I wasn't going to see her at my brother's house? If she thinks she can just ignore what's between us, she's wrong. I won't spend the next twelve years of my life wondering what if.

I will have a lot of groveling to do, but I know that once I get to see her in person again, there will be no backing away from her; she's mine. I just hope my angel will have mercy on me. Because she is my future.

I put my phone in my pocket and start packing up some of the remaining items in the house. I only have two more weeks until closing and need to donate a bunch of shit.

So, for right now, I'm just not going to think about Emmy; in a few hours, she won't be able to hide from me anyway. With that thought in mind, I smile and get to work.

* * *

I'm happy to see Emmy's car parked in the driveway at Ryan and Joanne's house as I pull up.

Good. I'll try and talk to her before I tell Ryan about us. After all, she can't be too mad at me for being here. I tried to tell her, but she's the one who is ignoring me now, not that I can really blame her for it; I was an ass.

I grab the bottle of wine from the passenger seat, now a little hesitant at my choice to bring wine as a gift after everything Joanne had said—there was a history of alcohol abuse in her family.

Although I do doubt she wouldn't have even served alcohol at her wedding if she had been the one who had the issues, right?

No going back now. I'm just going to hope for the best out of tonight.

Knocking on the front door, I wait a little nervously. I really want this evening to go well. I need this to go well.

Joanne answers the door with a big welcome smile. She's flanked by two dogs, tails wagging.

She wraps me in a hug. "I'm so glad you could make it."

"Thanks for having me." I smile back.

Reaching down and giving the pups some rubbing before standing back up to fully take in the woman in front of me.

I hadn't paid much attention to her before; I was a little focused on someone else at the wedding.

It was crazy how much Emmy looked like her mother; they had the same golden yellow hair and the same soft glow to their skin. Joanne's a little more tanned at the moment from her time in Belize. She also had little wrinkle lines starting to form next to her eyes, barely showing her age. She was only a year younger than myself and was most definitely a stunning woman.

The main difference in their appearances was that, unlike Emmy, Joanne had blue eyes, not honey brown.

I give her another smile and hand her the bottle of wine.

"I hope this is okay. I didn't want to come empty-handed."

"It's fine, thank you."

She takes the wine from me, grabs my arm, and leads me inside.

We are followed by the dogs as we walk through the home. It's so modern, all crisp lines, gray and white color pallets.

As we reached the kitchen area, the very modern interior continued; the counter was a bright white with stainless steel appliances. The bar stools at the kitchen island are a deep gray and stainless.

It was weird that this is the first time I've been in my brother's house. Of course, his appliances were the newest techy ones available; he has a fridge that can talk to you and tell you what's inside, kinda creepy if you ask me.

Joanne sets the wine down on the island before rounding it and squeezing Ryan from behind, standing on tiptoe so she can kiss him on the cheek. He was just pulling something that smelled delicious out of the oven.

Setting it on the stove above, he turns and hugs her, kissing her hair.

"Everyone is out on the patio," Joanne says while motioning to the large glass doors just off the kitchen.

My heart does a little pitter-patter in anticipation of seeing Emmy again. I didn't exactly leave things under the best of terms.

"I'll be out with the food in just a minute," Ryan adds.

I nod at them both and head to the patio. Slowly sliding the door open, stepping out into the evening air, dry and warm as usual for southern Utah, even in September. It wouldn't get colder until the sun went down.

I look to the far side of the patio, where a large rectangle table sits, with a fire pit in the center with colored glass. The fire pit isn't turned on, yet it's still visually pleasing.

There are people in conversation, drinking and eating some finger appetizers.

Scanning the people, I don't see Emmy among them. Joanne's parents, I recognize from the wedding; I met them briefly. A couple other people I had seen in passing at the wedding but haven't met yet, and toward the end of the table was Tonya.

What the fuck was she doing here? Her and Ryan weren't that close back in the day, so why is she everywhere now?

I turn to walk back in the house, hoping Emmy is in there somewhere; if I could bet, she's probably avoiding Tonya.

"Hey, Adrian." Tonya's highly feminine voice calls from behind me.

I pause while grabbing the door handle and turn with a fake smile on my face.

"Tonya."

She walks closer. Thankful she doesn't reach out to touch me; she stops in front of me.

"I just wanted to apologize for the wedding. I was out of line."

"Not the only time you've been out of line. Tonya, I have nothing to say to you." I keep my voice low, only for her to hear.

She looks at me, stunned that I would speak to her that way. Pulling the door back open, I step back inside.

Ryan was still in the kitchen; he was plating up some salmon and roasted bacon cauliflower with parmesan sauce. The food looked and smelled amazing; the aroma filled the large space.

"Why is Tonya here?" I don't wait to ask.

Ryan looks at me, bemused. "I kind of thought you two were getting along well."

I hadn't told him about what happened at the wedding with her; only briefly explained that Emmy was upset about something and had taken off when I asked for the tracking info, so yeah, guess he wouldn't have known about how Tonya was a royal bitch.

"Well, we aren't." I grit out, keeping my voice low enough that no one else would accidentally overhear.

Just thinking of how she had upset Emmy pisses me off. I know now that she wasn't the reason things between Sarah and I went south and ended the way they did, but I still can't get past her lies and venomous attitude, or the fact she knew the whole time Sarah wasn't being faithful and instead of telling me, she tried to seduce me. What was she going to gain from that?

Ryan holds up his hands. "Don't come at me."

"You're right, sorry, man." I shrug to my brother. "Been dealing with a lot."

He looks at me questioningly. "More so than usual?"

I rub a hand down my face. "Kind of, it's different now."

"I want to talk; now isn't great, obviously; let's get through dinner and we will talk." His look softens, taking on that protective brother one I've seen many times over the years.

I needed to talk to him that was evident; how he would feel after was something I wasn't sure about, and fuck, I still needed to see Emmy.

Her car is here, so she has to be here somewhere.

"Help me take these out," Ryan says.

I grab some of the plates, taking them to the outside table. Joanne joins us shortly after.

I take a seat as far away from Tonya as possible.

"Emmy not joining us?" I ask Joanne, who's sitting next to Ryan on the other side of me.

She shakes her head. "She's not here," she says before taking a bite of her salmon.

"Not here?" I question. "Isn't that her red Cresting in the driveway?"

Ryan answers as Joanne is still chewing her last bite of food.

"She left last week for Italy. She thought it would be better to park the car here instead of at her apartment."

She did what?

"Italy?" I try to keep my voice neutral.

"Last minute, she decided to go with Lucy for a bit; she said she was going to focus on her art," Joanne answers. "You met Lucy at the wedding, right?" she asks.

"I did; she was a sweet girl. I thought she didn't have to start school until next week."

"They left early so they could do some exploring together."

I do my best to keep my face neutral. I had so many more questions, but I couldn't ask them in front of everyone without making a big deal or revealing my relationship to everyone here. So, I settled myself internally.

"How fun."

I take a big bite of the roasted cauliflower. The creamy parmesan sauce mixed with the bacon and cauliflower has the perfect mix of smooth and savory with a little crunch. It's packed full of flavor. Who knew Ryan could cook like this?

"This is really good, Ryan."

"Yes, it is." Some of the other guests add.

"Oh, it wasn't me, that was all Joanne; I just pulled it out of the oven."

Joanne blushed a little pink, crossing her cheeks.

It makes me think of Emmy. I loved to watch her cheeks heat and the color of her porcelain skin change.

I can't believe she left without saying goodbye. That's not true; of course, she would leave without saying goodbye. I walked out of her apartment without saying goodbye and never called her.

What did I expect—she would just wait for me to get my shit together? Part of me had expected she would, even though she had told me she wouldn't be the one I used to fix myself. Well, I didn't need her to fix me; I was doing that on my own, like she suggested. It didn't change the fact I still needed her.

I continued the meal without adding much to the conversation. I listened to Joannes parents bickering back and forth about Dan, her dad, having an extra glass of whisky. I noted to myself that Dan must be the reason Joanne was concerned about how much Emmy had been drinking.

I also learned the other couple were Kelly and Kevin. Kevin worked for Ryan, none of which I cared about. My mind was far from here; I was just grateful. Tonya also stayed relatively quiet, only making small talk with the others. It's only when she goes to leave that she stops by me.

"Walk me out, please," Tonya asks, her voice holding a pleading sound.

To avoid a scene, I stand and walk in front of her until we are outside. Turning I glare at her.

"What could you possibly want to talk about, Tonya?"

I don't miss her body recoiling from me.

"I-I—*ugh*, I just wanted to say sorry."

"You already did that." I snap back.

She straightens a little.

"I mean for everything, I am sorry. I see now how horrible I have been all these years."

"If you think this is going to change anything with us, you are wrong."

"No. I don't. I just needed to get it off my chest. I am sorry. I behaved poorly in the past, and I knew Sarah wasn't good for you, and instead of just telling you, I tried to manipulate you to see I would be better."

Clenching my fists, I have to remember that I am moving on from this. I breathe in and let it out slowly.

"We are nothing, you understand? I don't want you anywhere near my life again."

A tear slips down her hard-composed face.

"I understand."

"Bye, Tonya."

"Goodbye, Adrian."

Leaving her standing in the driveway, I walk back to the house. Trying to stay calm, that woman gets on every nerve I have, and knowing for sure she had known about Sarah's infidelity doesn't make it easier.

After all the other guests have taken off, I follow Ryan into his home office.

It's not what you would typically imagine in an office; it doesn't have any dark wood furniture. It's modern like the rest of his house, with clean light colors, hard angles, and modern light furniture. The only pop of color came from a large painting on the side wall. It was a beautifully painted landscape of the Utah arches at sunset, the pink, reds, and oranges of the sky against the coppery red stone of the arch and the blue and dark of the mountains you could see in the distance.

It was a stunning piece.

Walking closer to the picture, I noticed the signature at the bottom. I knew she had talent; I had seen the girl in Shibari, but I had no idea she could do this. I think back to the two landscapes on her apartment walls; she must have done those too.

"Great work, right?" Ryan asks behind me.

"It's top tier, for sure."

"I was glad when she told us she wanted to spend some time in Italy. I haven't been in her life long, but she's seemed kind of lost since I met her. She has so much talent. I'd hate to see it wasted; I think this trip will be a good push for her."

I wanted to argue with him that she wasn't lost; she was just young and exploring, and I wanted to argue that she shouldn't be in Italy. I couldn't; he was right; she had talent, and I bet the pieces she would make in Italy would be equally amazing, and if I was being honest with myself, I didn't know her enough to know what she was truly feeling. Aside from our physical connection, did I really know what she wanted?

I had told myself years ago that I would never feel for anyone again, so why did it feel like a piece of my heart—a piece that I didn't know I still had—was being cut from me all over?

"So, what's got you in such a conundrum?" Ryan asks, taking a seat on his white leather couch.

It wouldn't do me any good to bring up Emmy now; she's not here to defend herself in the situation, so I settled with telling him about what I had found out about Sarah and how I was finally taking the proper steps to moving forward.

Emmy

Approximately a month later.

My stay in Italy has lasted longer than I had initially planned. I have been here for nearly six weeks now. I have had such an amazing time.

I don't know if I will ever get the opportunity to come back in the future, so I have taken full advantage of the time that I did have here.

On the days Lucy was out of school, we traveled all over the countryside together, visiting amazing towns and sites like the Coliseum, the Roman Forum, Venice, Verona, Tuscany, and everywhere you could think of. When she couldn't come with me, I traveled alone.

I explored the beautiful cliffside towns of Positano, Amalfi, Ravello, Maiori, and Minori along the Amalfi Coast.

They were all so incredible—whole cities built along the sea cliffs.

Trying all the local food has been another favorite thing I have loved to do. I have been craving the smells and flavors of everything I come across, so I tend to overindulge, and it hasn't always agreed with me.

Even surrounded by all the new and exciting places here, the hardest thing for me had still been trying to not wonder about Adrian. I have tried not to think about him, or how broken he had looked when he left that day. Yet I find myself constantly thinking about how he is doing.

In Minori, I met a really nice guy named Luca. He was everything I should have wanted to experience on a trip like this: twenty-five, handsome, sweet, and available, like something straight out of a romance novel. He spent two weeks showing me around and taking me to the less-- touristy places.

He was funny and made me laugh, and for a while, he had helped keep my mind off Adrian.

One evening, we walked along this old stone pathway along the cliffside above the ocean. We were enjoying the mist the ocean breeze brought up. The sun was low on the horizon and cast a beautiful glow across the water.

Luca turned me to him, gripping around my neck, pulling me close, leaning down, and kissed me. It was full of passion. I kissed him back, wanting to feel something—to feel that same passion he was putting into it as he devoured my mouth with his tongue.

But I didn't; the excitement—the butterflies; it wasn't there, my body hadn't reacted to him the way it had with Adrian. And when I closed my eyes, it wasn't Luca; I saw it was Adrian, and in that moment, it felt wrong to be there with Luca.

What should have been a picture-perfect magical moment just confirmed what I had been denying to myself: there wasn't another man out there that could make me feel the way Adrian had.

If I had only known at the time, would I have tried harder to keep him and not let him walk away so easily?

I don't know the answer to that.

What I had known all along was that he would ruin me, crush me, and break me. I just didn't know it would happen even without him there; I barely knew him.

It didn't seem to matter though; after all, there were a million stories and poems written about that one kind of love, the once in a lifetime, instant kind of love.

He was that for me, even if I couldn't be that for him.

When I had pulled back from Luca, he had known.

He remained ever the gentlemen, walking me back to the train that I needed to catch to make it back home.

Il cuore vuole quello che vuole, Luca had said to me before we parted ways.

I had to look up the words in the translation app I had been using; it roughly translated into 'The heart wants what it wants,' not sure if he meant mine or his, but it fit either way.

* * *

Today, being my last day in Italy, I was sitting on the steps of one of my favorite places to visit. The Milan Cathedral not only does it have the world's largest stained-glass windows, but it is also considered by many to be the best example of Gothic architecture in the world. It has 2,245 statues on the façade.

I have come here several times in the past month, catching the train from Florence, where we were living, to Milan. The fast train cut the over-three-hour trip down to just over an hour and a half.

The cathedral is where most of the inspiration for my paintings have come from while I've been here. It has an energy; I can't explain how it feels, just that I love it.

I have been fortunate enough to sell a few pieces to tourists who have stumbled across me as I worked. It was a nice way to make my trip more relaxed, not having to worry about funds or being a burden to Lucy.

I wasn't painting today though; I was just taking it all in before I had to go home and back to reality.

I am going to miss it here; even the slight chill in the early autumn air is something I'm going to miss. Italy is just so magical.

It had opened up its heart to me, and I had fallen in love with it; it had given me that sense of something more I was looking for. I was going home with a plan for my future.

Lucy will be meeting me in Milan shortly to eat my last meal here at one of the amazing rooftop restaurants that overlooks the city and the cathedral. A goodbye dinner with my best friend.

"I wish you were staying longer; it's been so great to have you here," Lucy declares.

"I know. Thank you for letting me tag along."

Lucy reaches across the table and squeezes my hand.

"So, tell me, what do you have planned for when you get back to Utah?"

"Ugh, I don't know." I let out a long sigh.

"Well, you know Jimmy will be there when you get back; he ended up completing his PA and took a job at a Dr. office in town."

"Really, he didn't want to stick it out longer to get his full doctorate?"

She shrugs. "I don't know why he did it, but he says he's happy with his choice, so I'm happy for him."

"Good for him."

"Have you talked to Adrian?" Lucy asks.

I have avoided any conversation pertaining to him since we have been here. Lucy still believes in fate and fairytales; she hasn't seen the darkness the world really has.

"No, why would I? I tried to see him before we left. His house was up for sale, and he clearly didn't want to talk to me because he didn't even send me a text to tell me. I even went by the bar once, but he wasn't there either."

"Okay, but."

"No, but Lucy; he left, didn't try to talk to me, so why do I owe him anything? I don't know if he is even in the state anymore."

"I think you love him, Emmy. In fact, I know you do. I just hate you're hurting."

"I don't know what to do." I hold back the wave of emotion that rocks me with her words. I don't know how it's possible to fall for someone so quickly, but I had.

If only my caring for him was enough to fix whatever messed up thing was between us.

He was broken inside; I didn't know if he was capable of loving someone else, and I know that even with all the work I have done to be enough for myself, I can't fix him.

"Don't start crying on me," Lucy says.

"Sorry. I can't help it." I wipe a fallen tear. "What am I going to do without you there with me?"

"I'll be back for summer break; it's only like six months away."

"You better be." Waving to stop where the conversation was going.

"Enough with me. Tell me how class is going."

"It's so great!" She practically squeals with excitement as she goes into detail about the techniques and dishes she's already learning to make.

"So far, my favorite is acorn squash stuffed with orzo and pancetta. The instructor is an ass though."

I laugh. "I thought you said he was hot."

"He is. He's hot, Italian, and an asshole." She's still grinning as she stuffs another bite of her risotto in her mouth.

"Well, hot assholes must be our new thing."

She snorts and has to catch the food she was still chewing in her hand.

We are both laughing so hard that most of the eyes in the restaurant are looking at us.

"Sorry, *Spiacente*," I say loud enough for the people around us to hear and stuff a ravioli in my mouth.

"I am not even going there," Lucy says.

"Okay, whatever you say, but hot assholes are a good bang."

"I'll take your word for it."

Shrugging, I finished up my plate of ravioli.

Once I have devoured every morsel off my plate, I call for the waiter to come over so I can order desserts.

Per favóre, posso avere la cheesecake al tiramisu, I ask in Italian, having been practicing and hoping I didn't just butcher it.

Ma Certo, he replies and heads off to put in the desert order.

"You're really going to eat dessert after all that pasta?" Lucy comments.

"Don't underestimate the fat kid inside of me."

Knowing full well it will probably not sit well after I'm done, I'm going to enjoy every bite of it anyway.

"Never." She laughs.

The waiter returns with the most amazing-looking cheesecake I have ever seen. It's like cheesecake on steroids.

After a couple delectable bites, I set my fork down. "I can't eat another bite."

Lucy gives me a sideways look and grin.

"Told ya. You aren't even close to finishing it."

As I was trying to think of a witty reply, the nausea took over quicker than I had expected. Bolting up from the table barely, making it into the stall, I shove the door aside, heaving my beautifully made dinner and dessert into the toilet bowl.

Once done emptying my stomach of its contents, I wash and head back to the table.

"Well, that sucked." I huff, plopping back into my chair.

"Have you maybe thought about why you keep doing..." I cut her off before she could finish her sentence. I know what she is going to say, and I don't want to hear it.

"Not going there."

"It's about time for us to leave anyway," Lucy says, her voice cracking. "I'm really going to miss having you here."

"I'm going to miss being here with you."

* * *

Sixteen hours later, I'm waiting outside the Vegas airport for my mom to pick me up.

I tried to tell her I could take the shuttle, but she insisted on making the two and a half-hour drive to pick me up.

Pulling my phone out and turning it on for the first time in six weeks; I hadn't used it since I left. While in Italy, I just used a pre-pay so I didn't get crazy roaming or international charges, and the only person I talked to was my mom.

I wasn't expecting any notifications, as I had stayed in contact with her almost daily while I was gone, and Lucy wouldn't have called me yet.

Three missed calls and four messages come across my screen.

Adrian: Can we talk?
Adrian: Emmy, please; I need to talk to you.

The first two were a week after I left, two weeks after Adrian had walked out my door. It feels like a lifetime ago now, yet seeing them makes my heart hurt all over again.

Scrolling down, I read the next two messages. The first one is from a week ago.

Adrian: I'm still pissed at you. I can't believe you left like this. I don't know what to do.

He's pissed at me?

The last one was only from yesterday.

Adrian: Angel, I know our time together has been short, but every minute I spent with you was better than any day I've had in years. I know our story isn't over yet, and I want to see what comes next.

Even in his silly rambling, he makes me smile. I clutch my phone to my chest.

Where do we go from here?

Where do I even want it to go?

I had resolved myself to the fantastical idea that he would be a fond memory, one thought about years from now when I had grown and moved on. The one who would cross my mind as the one who got away but taught me so much. The one who had paved the way for the life I would eventually build.

Adrian

I've been driving myself crazy pacing the guest room at Ryan's house.

It's been weeks of me staying here, since after the sale of my house I hadn't wanted to buy anything else, not without first finding out where I stood with Emmy.

If she was really done with me, I'd leave and go back to Oregon, but if there was a chance she'd consider something with me, I needed to know.

I have called and texted her several times since she left; her phone has been off the whole time.

I had to talk myself out of jumping on a damn plane to get to her more than once during the past month, but I needed to give her space after what I did to her.

But my self-control was wearing thin, and if Joanne hadn't told me a few days ago that she was going to be home today, I probably would have given in, and flown my ass to Italy.

I was ashamed of how I acted that last day. How I treated her was wrong.

I knew she was physically okay from her calls to Joanne. That didn't keep me from worrying, I needed to see her; I needed to touch her. At this point, she seems like a figment of my imagination, someone I made up, a perfect angel sent just to me in a dream.

There was so much left unsaid between us; I had fucked her on a fucking counter and just left after. What kind of fucked-up person does that?

I had looked into her innocent eyes, filled with pain, and just walked away.

I had to find a way to make it right; I fucking needed her more than I wanted to admit. Without even trying, she slid her way into my heart; she was so open and willing to be with me, and I used it.

"Fuck."

Knock knock

I look over to the door; it opens, whoever is behind it, not waiting for my reply after knocking.

"You good?"

Ryan walks in, filling the space between the door and me. "You're going to wear a path on my floor, from what I can hear."

I look at him, a little embarrassed.

"Sorry, man."

"I haven't pressed because I know you're finally working through shit but…" he trails off, running his hand on the back of his neck. "But you seem different. Something you want to talk about?"

"Nothing I know how to talk about," I say honestly.

"Okay, well, I'm here, ya know. Just because we are adults doesn't mean I'm not here for you, little brother."

Ryan looks at me concerned but doesn't say anything else as he turns to leave the room.

"Hey."

He stops in the doorway, hand on the frame.

"Thanks."

Giving me a small smile and a nod of his head before he walks out.

This shit was getting to me. I wish I could talk to Ryan about it.

Joanne left hours ago to pick up Emmy from the airport. If it wouldn't have been a weird request, I would have asked to go myself or at least to tag along.

Instead, I'm here, pacing my borrowed room like a maniac.

I really want to talk to Emmy first. I don't want to start unnecessary family drama if she doesn't want to give me a chance. The constant battle I had been fighting in my mind on being the bigger person and walking away or staying was killing me.

My therapist had been helping me let go of the past and move forward. So here I was, still sitting at my brother's house, counting on getting that face-to-face talk with Emmy before it's too late.

Emmy

The windshield wipers swish back and forth as the rain patters on the windows on our drive toward home.

The dreary weather felt like a reflection of how I was feeling inside.

My unease increased as the miles passed, getting closer and closer to home.

His texts were one thing; him a complete other. He left without saying goodbye; he sold his house. I don't even know what his plan is, yet he's mad at me for leaving.

Do I dare ask my mom about him?

I look over at her, and she smiles sideways at me.

"I'm so happy you're back."

"Me too, Mom."

Surprisingly, I mean it. I am happy to be back home. I loved Italy, but it didn't feel like home.

"It's going to be weird without Lucy here."

"I'm sure; you two have been thick as thieves forever. How's she liking school?"

"Loving it; she won't admit it, but she has the hots for her teacher." I tease.

My mom laughs. "Oh, no."

"Yeah, I haven't seen him personally, but the way Lucy talks about him, I think she's got it bad."

We spent the next half hour talking about all the things I loved in Italy.

The rain doesn't lighten up the entire drive; normally, I love the rain, but today it was adding a melancholy feel.

"Thanks for coming to get me; sorry, you're driving in this rain."

"Don't worry about it, honey; we're not too far now."

"So now that we've talked all about me, tell me what's new with you?"

"Nothing exciting, loving married life."

"That makes me happy, Mom. I'm so glad you found a good one."

"He really is; he doesn't even complain when Tank and Zeek hog the bed from us."

"Aww, that's sweet."

"How's everyone else been?"

"Grandpa is stubborn as usual; Grandma has been doing her normal bingo nights, and has dragged me along a few times."

"Good."

I wish I could just ask her outright about Adrian. I purse my lips together.

"Are you staying for dinner when we get back or heading straight home?"

"Not sure; I haven't eaten anything in hours; the food on the plane wasn't great." As if in agreement, my stomach makes a rumbling noise.

"I am looking forward to showering and getting some sleep, though. I'm exhausted."

"Well, you probably don't have any food at home, so you might as well eat with us. I can make up the office if you want to crash there tonight; that way, you can have breakfast in the morning too, which gives you time to go get some groceries tomorrow."

"That's probably a good idea. Why the office, though? What are you doing in the spare room?"

"Oh, I forgot to mention Adrian's been staying with us; he sold his house, and while he's looking for something else, he's been staying at our place. Ryan has really loved having him around."

My heart sinks. Yeah, I wanted to know about him; I just didn't think I'd be confronted with him at my mom's house the second we arrive.

I have to tamp down a wave of nausea. My body shivers. Do I want to see him? Yes, of course I do, but how do I do that right in front of my mom?

"You okay? Do I need to turn up the heat?"

"I'm fine; I think jet lag is getting to me. I don't know if I'm up for a family dinner."

She eyes me but doesn't say whatever it is she's thinking.

"Do you think you could just swing in somewhere to get some food then take me home?"

"If that's what you really want to do."

"I don't know; I'm just tired."

I can't very well tell her I'm internally panicking at the thought of seeing Adrian again after nearly two months. Maybe he won't even say anything to me, and then I'm pulled back to his last text, he said he wants more.

How? Is that what I want? I don't want to get hurt worse than I already am; right now, he isn't anything to me. If I try for more, what will happen to my heart when it ends then?

I wish I could talk to my mom about it.

"Something on your mind, sweety?"

I watch the rain pool in little droplets and slide down the window, war-ing with myself on what to say.

"A lot, really, but I don't know how to talk about it."

"Is it about that guy you met in Italy?"

Of course, that's where she would go with this; I completely forgot. I even told her about Luca on one of our calls.

"Kind of, but not fully."

"Well, you know you can talk to me, right?"

It's hard for me to talk to her like this. She is a great mom, but she has always been a little selfish too, which I totally get. I can't imagine having a kid so young and losing everything she had wanted for her future. It's only in the past few years that our relationship has gotten better, I think once the real pressure of being a mom was off when I became an adult is when she truly started to change how she was with me. Like I was no longer a burden to her. I love her, and I know she loves me always has, but I also knew some part of her resented me too, not that she would ever admit it. And as a kid, that was hard.

"Have you ever thought about having more kids?" I ask her, wondering if now that she has her life together if she would want a true family with Ryan.

I watch the expressions on her face change.

"I love you, you know that right?"

"Of course, I do, Mom. That's not why I was asking."

"I did the best I knew how to do with you. I know I wasn't always the greatest at it, but every choice I made was something I did to try and make your life better." The pain is evident in her voice.

I reach out and touch her shoulder.

"Mom, I know it was. You were just a kid too; you did a good job. I was happy and cared for; I finished school with honors. You gave me everything a kid needs."

"Thanks, sweety."

"I was just wondering if you and Ryan had talked about starting your own little family."

She lets out a small laugh. "You don't think that would be weird?"

"Of course not; I know lots of people who wait until your age to have kids."

"That may be true, but I already have one, and you're getting to the age where you might find someone and have one or two of your own."

"Yeah, but look how I turned out. I can only imagine how amazing you'd do the second time around with someone who wants to do it with you."

A silent tear slips down her cheek.

"You wouldn't feel like I was replacing you?"

"Absolutely not."

"It would be kind of fun to have a little one around again, do holiday stuff like trick or treating."

"If it's something you guys decide on, just know I'm good, okay?"

"Thank you." She squeezes my thigh.

"This isn't what's been bothering you, though; I know it's something else. You may be an adult, but I'm still your mother, and I know when something has you upset."

Sighing I know it might be a good time to tell her about Adrian, since I've already kept it a secret for so long. I'm too much of a coward to do that, though, so instead I tell her a smaller version of the truth.

The rest of the now-short drive to her place I tell her what really happened to my face the night before her wedding. I tell her about the guy who saved me. I leave out the part of who it was or the fact I went home with him like a little slut.

I do tell her how it's complicated that he has some baggage that I'm not sure he can get through, and that basically I couldn't get him off my mind the entire trip.

I also leave out the other little secret, the one I haven't even confirmed myself, but have suspected for a couple weeks.

"Well, you're an adult and can make your own choices. Just don't settle for anything less than you deserve." She looks over at me and gives me a small smile. "If he's right for you, he will make you the priority. You deserve more than a heartache."

After the heart-to-heart with my mom, I decided to send off a text to Adrian.

Me: We do need to talk. But not tonight, please.
Adrian: Whatever you need, Angel.

I'm mentally, emotionally, and physically exhausted by the time we pull into the driveway.

I hope that Adrain keeps his distance. I don't know if I'm capable of doing it myself. No matter how amazing Italy was, I still fell asleep each night thinking about him, wishing I could share with him all the places I got to visit, and wondering how it was so easy for him to ghost me like he did.

I know it sounds stupid and I shouldn't care so much about him so soon, but I do. I did, and, until three hours ago, I thought he didn't feel the same. Now what do I do with the knowledge that maybe he thought about me this whole time too?

Adrian

Ryan is in the kitchen, prepping a small dinner, when I finally venture from the spare room.

"What ya got going on in here?"

"Joanne called a bit ago; they are almost here. She mentioned that Emmy was a bit jet lagged and didn't want to make a big fuss with dinner and all."

"Makes sense; that's a big time difference, and the flights are long as shit."

"Yeah, so I thought I'd stick to something simple: salad, and chicken breasts."

"Need any help?"

"Think I'm good; thanks though."

Grabbing a drink out of the fridge, I take a seat on one of the bar stools.

Popping the tap, I take a nice, long gulp of the refreshing liquid.

"Thought they would be back already."

"Got slowed down by the rain; Joanne called a bit ago and said the storm was basically the whole way."

"Huh, hadn't even noticed the rain." I shrug. Glancing outside.

The rain here seems to be just a drizzle now.

"Do you know what you're going to do about your own place yet?"

"Hey, thanks for letting me stay here. I know that's not super romantic as a newlywed couple to have your brother staying with you."

"Not why I asked ya goof."

"Just saying, thanks." I pause, then add, "I'll get my own place soon or just head back to Oregon and get out of your hair."

Ryan sets down the knife he was using to chop up some olives for the salad.

"I was hoping you'd stay closer. It's been nice to have you back. Even though something else has been on your mind. You have been a lot more you over the past couple months."

"Yeah I know what you mean. I started counseling right after all that shit came out about Sarah. It's really helped me let go in a way."

"Good for you, brother."

Ryan goes back to cutting up things and tossing them in a bowl. I take another big gulp of my drink. Getting the nerve to finally tell Ryan about Emmy.

It might be better for me to talk to him alone anyway.

"I met someone I'm really interested in," I start.

His eyes shoot up, and smirking grin crosses his face—the kind that crinkles your eyes.

"I suspected." He chuckles.

Don't know if he'll continue that chuckle in a minute.

Bzzzzzz

The vibration notification of my phone gives me a breather to come up with a delicate way to word what I want to say.

Angel: We do need to talk. But not tonight, please.
Me: Whatever you need, Angel.

The initial excitement of seeing the text from her quickly fades into something else—fear, sadness—I'm not sure. I won't push her; I can be patient. I have waited two months already; what's another day?

"That your girl?" He gestures toward the phone.

"Hopefully." I shrug.

"If she's someone you can't see life without, don't squander it."

"I've just made a few mistakes already, and I'm not sure how to fix them."

"Be honest."

Fifteen minutes later, the sound of the garage door opening has me on my feet.

Instinctively, I gravitate to the side door in the kitchen, the one that leads to the garage. Stopping myself halfway there, what am I doing? I'm not some eager teenager; I'm a grown ass man.

Joanne is chattering away to Emmy as they push open the door.

I hold in a breath as she finally steps through the doorway. Her golden hair is pulled up in a loose half ponytail; strands of it fall out around her face; no makeup on; she's wearing an oversized sweatshirt with the neck cut wide that hangs halfway off one shoulder and leggings. She is absolutely beautiful.

When she finally lifts her face to me, we lock eyes. Her honey brown eyes glisten with unshed tears.

The same pained look on her face as the last time I saw her, when I left her standing in her apartment.

She takes in an audible breath.

Lowering her gaze.

It takes all I have not to walk over there and wrap her in my arms, tuck the hair out of her face, and tell her it's all going to be okay.

Ryan hurries over, giving Joanne a quick kiss on the cheek. And taking the bag from Emmy's hand.

"Thank you," Emmy says softly to Ryan.

"Welcome home," he says as he takes her bag.

He turns to walk it down the hall, taking it to the office room. Joanne follows after him, leaving Emmy and I alone in the kitchen.

Trying to give her space, I walk back to the bar stool and wait for her to say or make a move.

"Dinner will be ready in a minute," Ryan calls from down the hall.

I watch Emmy as she walks to the fridge, grabbing a bottle of water. Still facing the fridge, her hands shake as she twists the lid off. If I hadn't been watching her so intently, I probably wouldn't have noticed it.

Standing, I walk up behind her, looking over my shoulder to make sure Ryan and Joanne aren't on their way back yet.

I can't help but feel excited to have her near me again. I've been going crazy with her gone.

"You okay, Angel?" I whisper into her ear.

The water sprays out the top in a rush as she squeezes the bottle crushing the sides, at the same time she jumps and screams, startled.

Shit, not what I was trying to do.

The water covers her, splashing onto my front too.

"I'm sorry. I didn't mean to scare you."

"Well, you did."

"Shit," she mumbles, looking at the water mess.

Ryan and Joanne come running in from the hall.

"What happened?" Ryan asks, looking over the scene in front of him.

I take a step back, realizing how close I am to Emmy.

"Sorry, I'm a bit jumpy."

"It was my fault; I went to grab the salad dressing out for dinner." I lied as an explanation.

Ryan eyes me a scowl on his face, and Joanne jumps into action, snatching up a towel to clean the mess.

"No, it was my fault I was spaced out and blocking the fridge; I didn't even hear Adrian come up."

"No harm done," Joanne says as she wipes up the floor.

"Mom, I could have done that."

Joanne waves off Emmy with a nonsense gesture. "I can clean up a little water."

Emmy

I'm in a better mood after talking to my mom, even if it wasn't the whole truth, it was nice to get some of it off my chest. It weighed me down the entire trip.

After she found out about the incident with the guy in the parking lot, she was a little pissed at me for not saying something sooner. I assured her it was all handled. We are still in a light chatter as we enter the house. For a minute, I had forgotten Adrian might be here.

Stepping through the door, I let my mom go in ahead of me, looking up, walking in, and shutting the door behind me.

For the first time since he left me standing in my apartment, I'm looking into the eyes of Adrian. His mesmerizing hazel eyes are the same intense colors I remember—the very ones that haunt my dreams.

His muscled body tense. I can tell he's holding himself back; there is tightness in his arms and shoulders.

Looking at him, I see the lost, broken soul who walked away from me.

The ache in my chest returns. At that moment, all the feelings from that day came rushing back; I inhaled an audible breath.

Lowering my eyes from him, holding back tears that threaten to run down my face, unwelcome.

Ryan rushes over, giving my mom a kiss on the cheek. Reaching for the bag I have clutched in my hands, I let him take it.

"Thank you."

"Welcome home," he says before he heads down the hall to put my bag in the office.

My mom follows him out of the kitchen, leaving me alone with Adrian.

"Dinner will be ready in a minute," Ryan calls from down the hall.

All the nerves from before shiver through my body. Walking to the fridge, I grab a bottle of water.

Still facing the fridge to chickenshit to turn around, I twist the lid off with shaking hands.

Thinking about all the things that I want to say to him. And remember the little plastic stick in my bag that I've been too scared to look at since I peed on it in the airport bathroom before boarding the plane.

I take a deep, calming breath.

A shiver runs down my spine as the fresh air and lemon mix that is Adrian reaches me.

"You okay, Angel?" Adrian whispers in my ear.

I scream from his unexpected nearness and squeeze the water bottle, causing the water to fountain out the top, covering me and probably Adrian with how close he was standing to me.

"I'm sorry. I didn't mean to scare you."

"Well, you did."

"Shit." There is water puddling at my feet, dripping from my hair, and covering my sweatshirt. I look over at Adrian, who has managed to escape most of the water, only a splattering of wetness on him.

Ryan and my mom come running into the kitchen.

"What happened?" Ryan asks, looking over the scene in front of him.

Adrian takes a step back. I winch.

"Sorry, I'm a bit jumpy," I offer an explanation.

"It was my fault; I went to grab the salad dressing out for dinner," Adrian adds.

Ryan scowls at him. I wonder what that's about.

My mom, of course, doesn't miss a beat; she quickly retrieves a towel and gets to work, soaking up the watery mess.

"No, it was my fault, I was spaced out and blocking the fridge; I didn't even hear Adrian come up."

"No harm done."

"Mom, I could have done that."

She waves me off with her nonsense gesture. "I can clean up a little water."

"All better," she says, standing, setting the towel on the counter.

"Sorry," I say again.

"Come, let's eat so you can shower and get some rest," my mom says as she wraps an arm around my shoulder.

"Let me go take off this wet shirt first. I'll be right back."

Quickly running into the office, I strip off the wet sweatshirt and grab a t-shirt out of my bag. Throwing it on, I head back to the kitchen.

Sitting at the table is going to be harder than I thought. Ryan and my mom are sitting next to each other, so unless I want to raise more questions by sitting a few chairs down, I'm stuck taking the seat across from them, the one next to Adrian.

I'm thankful the table is not glass; the solid surface hides the nervous shake of my leg.

Taking a big bite of my chicken, I almost choke on it as Adrian places his hand on my thigh, stopping my leg from shaking.

Now I have to focus on chewing and taking small breaths in between bites to keep the neutral look on my face.

Adrian has no trouble staying in conversation as he rubs gentle circles up and down my thigh.

I, on the other hand, feel like I'm floating away. So much for having some space from him tonight. This man clearly has no self-control.

"So, Emmy, what's your plan now that you're back?" Ryan asks.

Back to earth…

"*Ughm*, I was thinking about looking into a studio space to open a gallery, maybe even somewhere closer to Vegas. Somewhere, I could get more foot traffic."

"So far?" my mom asks.

Adrains hand stops its exploration on my thigh.

"Just something I was thinking about; nothing is decided yet."

"I think it's great you're wanting to open your own gallery," Ryan says, showing genuine interest.

"Thanks." I smile.

I glance over at Adrian; he's studying his half-eaten plate of food. Clearly thinking something over in his head.

I want to ask him what's on his mind.

"I bet there are some great places around here that you could find," my mom chimes in.

"That's possible too, Mom. I just got back. I haven't even looked yet." I smile at her.

"Ryan could even help you set up a website, so you don't have to pay those high commissions on that site you use now to sell your pieces."

"That would be…" I begin to reply when Adrian interrupts before I can finish what I'm saying.

"You sell your art online?"

Looking over at him puzzled, giving him a what the hell look.

"Yeah, I use an art auction site to list them through; that's how I paid for my trip to Italy."

His face takes on more serious features; he has a tight scowl.

I blink in confusion before turning back to Ryan and my mom.

"That would be great, Ryan, if you have the time to do it."

"Of course, Emmy, I'd love to help you build your own site."

"Did you sell the shibari?" Adrian questions, physically turning in his chair toward me and pulling on my arm so I have to face him again.

Shock has me gasping, throwing a hand to cover my mouth, and heat immediately flushes my cheeks.

I know my eyes are as big as saucers when I look over at him.

What the actual fuck is he thinking? I cannot believe he is asking about that painting now.

"The what?" my mom asks, confused looking back and forth between me and Adrian.

Adrian, seemingly realizing his mistake, drops the hand that was gripping my upper arm.

Clearing his throat.

"Just a painting I saw when I checked on Emmy after the wedding. It was a stunning piece."

Thankfully, my mom has probably never heard of Shibari.

"All her stuff is great," she says.

I can feel tension in the air that wasn't there before. I glance over toward Ryan, who hasn't said a word. He's stiff and has an unreadable face, staring daggers at his brother.

My mom is blissfully unaware.

I feel sick.

Taking a large bite of chicken, chewing, trying to think of a way out of this, and hoping the chicken stays down.

Ryan clearly isn't as unaware as my mom; he seems to be suspecting something. Even before that remark, he was being a little apprehensive toward Adrian.

I think back on the look he gave Adrian when I spilled the water. I don't know what Ryan might think, but it's probably not good.

Taking the fork and stabbing it into the remainder of the chicken, I try to finish off my plate in a hurry.

I want to escape this disaster waiting to happen.

"So, Emmy, your mom tells me you met someone in Italy?" Ryan asks me, but his focus is still on Adrian; my guess is he's watching for his reaction.

I give Adrian credit; he didn't even flinch like I did at his question.

"Yeah, Luca, he was a great tour guide," I say as plainly as possible.

"Any plans to keep in touch now that you're back?"

I shake my head. "No, I haven't talked to him in a week or so."

My mom looks up at Ryan. Confusion on her face.

"I told you that didn't work out. Remember?" she asks him.

"Oh, yes, sorry. I must have forgotten. My mistake." He smiles at her and looks back at me.

"I'm going to turn in," I say, pushing back from the table, standing, I grab my plate to take it to the sink.

Adrian stands and, at the same time, I hold my breath.

"You've had a long day; let me take that for you."

He reaches for the plate, and reluctantly, I hand it to him.

"Thanks."

Rushing down the short hallway, I practically run to the bathroom, shutting the door behind me. I sit on the toilet, gasping in breaths, body shaking. I feel like I'm going to have a panic attack.

Then the nausea comes over me, slipping off the seat. I throw the lid up; the sound of the porcelain hitting each other echoes in the small space, and I heave the dinner back up.

As I'm washing up, there's a small knock at the door.

"Is everything okay in there?"

I'm surprised it's Ryan and not my mom's voice I hear on the other side of the door.

"Fine."

Slowly, I open the door, plastering a fake smile on.

Ryan's eyes soften as he looks at me. I know I look disheveled. Redness on my neck and cheeks, damp hair, and puffy eyes.

"You sure you're all right?"

"I'm fine, thank you. It's just been a really long day."

He looks at me sympathetically.

"I know I haven't been in your life long, Emmy, and I'm sure I'm the last person you want to talk to; just know if you need to. I'm here, okay."

I give him a quick hug.

"Thank you, Ryan."

He's thrown off by the unexpected gesture, and he lightly pats my back.

"Of course, hun."

"Where's Mom?" I ask, looking down the hall.

"She went upstairs already. I think that drive wore her out too." He smiles again.

He smiles anytime he talks about or looks at my mom, and that makes me happy.

"Ya, I know I'm going to crash. I don't know how I haven't passed out yet."

"Get some sleep," he says before walking away.

Heading to the office, I forgo the shower, changing into some sweats. The white leather couch has been covered in a sheet with a blanket and pillow.

I just have to do one more thing before I can sleep.

Shuffling through my bag, I grab the brown paper sack that holds the plastic stick out and take a seat on the couch.

I sit there, just holding the sack. I don't know if I want to open it to confirm what I already think it will say.

Lucy joked with me about it a couple weeks ago, but she hadn't known at the time that it was an actual possibility. She had said my appetite had changed and mentioned the nausea I got almost every time I ate.

I had attributed it to the different types of foods and definitely the overeating, I had stuffed my face any chance I got on that trip, I'm surprised I didn't gain a ton of weight.

I had brushed it off; I had gotten a period while there; it was a light one, but I thought, *No way.* Stress can cause the same reactions, after all, and Adrian was careful; he had used a condom every time he was inside of me the night I went home with him.

The only other time we had been together since then was when he took me in the kitchen. I hadn't thought much about it at the time or after, but he hadn't used one then. It was wild, hard, and fast, and I don't think either of us was in the right frame of mind at that moment.

I hadn't even thought it a possibility that I could have ended up knocked up. Not until Lucy joked about it. Wouldn't that be my luck—the one and only time I had been with someone without protection.

One thing I knew for sure was that if I am pregnant, it would be different from my mom and my relationship. One, I'm not sixteen, and I have more support than she did, even if I had to do this without Adrian. Also, I had a plan for my career with my art. I could support the baby and myself on my own.

Growing up, I didn't know if I even wanted kids, and I don't know Adrian well enough to know if he wants kids either, especially now.

This isn't ideal by any means, but whatever the outcome, I would make it work, and I wouldn't make the mistake of letting people in and out of my kid's life, not that I blame my mom fully. I know she did her best, but I don't think she knows what that does to a kid.

The first thing I needed to do was actually look in the damn bag.

With trembling fingers, I reach into the small brown bag, wrapping my hand around the small plastic stick, pulling it from the sack. The paper crinkles as I toss it aside.

Holding the stick, I turn it over, getting ready to look at the result screen.

Sucking in all the air I can, filling my lungs almost to the point of pain, I close my eyes, heart pounding in my chest. Just as I'm about to open my eyes and look down at the words, loud voices sound just outside the room.

Not thinking, still gripping the test, I bolt to the door, flinging it open.

Ryan has Adrian pinned to the wall directly across from me.

"When?" Ryan grits out.

I can see the anger rolling through him, his shoulders tight, and the grip he has on Adrian deadly.

"Oh, my god." I gasp at the scene in front of me.

Adrian

After dinner, I wanted to go straight to Emmy to make sure she was okay. She was visibly upset at dinner, and I didn't know what I was thinking, asking about that painting.

I just couldn't let someone else have it; the jealousy and anger had taken over. That damn painting was hers, and no one but me should see her that way.

I was going to have to find a way to buy it from whoever had it now.

Joanne had excused herself shortly after Emmy and headed up to bed.

The woman was kind of infuriating, the way she didn't seem to read her daughter's mood. It was both a good thing and one that pissed me off. She, of all the people in this house, should realize there is something going on with Emmy.

I know I was at least part of what Emmy's issues, but there was more. I could tell something else was going on with her.

I wanted to hold her, find out, and make sure she knew I would be there for her, no matter what. If that kid in Italy hurt her he was dead.

I had to wait until I thought Ryan had gone off to bed too. He had hung out downstairs long after I had come back to the room, and I knew he suspected something was up.

I could have just text her; however, my body needed to see her, and she was just down stairs, in the same house. I wouldn't be happy with just a text right now, and I needed to see her face, her eyes, and breathe in that scent of wildflowers.

Quietly, I make my way out the guest room, walking down the dark hallway.

My heart rate picks up only feet from the office door. I know she's still awake; the light from the office is still on, slipping out under the closed door.

"What the fuck are you doing?"

Turning, I am face-to-face with Ryan.

I hold up my hands in front of me, not wanting to fight with him. I know this looks bad. But he doesn't understand.

"Hey, brother, let me explain." Keeping my tone low.

"You better start talking, and it better be good." His words come out harsh, and it has me stepping back a few steps. Ryan has never taken that tone with me before.

"Look, this wasn't something I planned. I didn't even know who she was when I met her." I ramble out.

Not expecting it, I didn't have time to block as Ryan's fist connected to the side of my jaw. My head jerks sideways, pain shooting up the side of my face. His second attempt, I catch him, and he uses his body force to shove me back into the wall. I lose my grip on his hand.

I could try to swing back, but I won't. The last thing I want is to get into a fist fight with my brother.

"What you just think, oh, sweet another conquest, let me just take my brother's new step daughter home from his wedding while she's injured and vulnerable and have my way with her. Add her to your endless list of woman you fuck; consequences be damned," he spits out.

His words cut deep into me emotionally as his big frame pushed into me physically, gripping onto me with a deadly force I didn't know he had.

He must work out more than I had thought; he has me pinned to the wall, one arm sideways across my chest and the other around my throat.

"I met her before your wedding." I try to breathe; it comes out heavily as I'm trying to keep him from crushing my windpipe.

He releases my throat but doesn't relieve the pressure he has on my chest, still pressing me to the hard wall.

"When?" He grits out.

It's then that the light in the hall gets brighter, and the office door flings open. Looking over Ryan's shoulder, I can see Emmy silhouetted in the door.

"Oh, my god." She gasps.

Ryan looks over his shoulder, noticing Emmy. He drops his hold on me, and I fall forward slightly, hands on my knees, as I catch myself.

He walks toward her, and I stand quickly, pulling him back from getting to her.

"Stop it," she says, looking at both of us.

"Are you okay? Did he hurt you? Did he cause the bruises?" Ryans string of questions come out fast and accusative. Like he's just made this huge realization.

Is he for real? He thinks I would do something like that.

"NO," we both shout at the same time.

"I would never hurt her," I add.

She draws back a little. Damn it, that isn't true. I did hurt her, just not physically.

"He didn't do it; he stopped the guy who did," Emmy says with a quiver in her voice.

"He's the guy?" Joannes' voice practically echoes through the hall. We all turn to her; she's standing at the end of the hall, a robe wrapped around her.

She rushes over, and I don't even stop her as she starts pounding on my chest.

"Mom, stop!" Emmy screeches.

Running toward us, dropping something as she pulls her mom away from me.

Ryan takes hold of Joanne and pulls her into his chest as she cries.

"I'm sorry I didn't tell you, Mom. I didn't know how." Tears stream down Emmy's face.

Ryan looks at me. "Get out," he doesn't yell; nonetheless, it was still a command.

I go to step up next to Emmy, who's standing there staring at her mom and Ryan. That's when I notice the thing she dropped on the floor. I recognize what it is immediately; it's like the light from the office was illuminating it for me. There is no mistaking the little screen says: pregnant.

I drop to my knees and grab the little plastic stick. Oh god, like a flashback—the deleted pictures and text form Sarah's phone. The picture of the positive test, the confirmation from the Dr., the text back and forth from the guy she was seeing behind my back, the other possible father, the one she clearly thought was the father she had told him, she hadn't told me. All the images rush through my mind as I stare at the pregnancy test in my hand.

Who was the father of this baby? The guy she met in Italy?

My heart rate picks up, and my chest feels like it was put in a vice grip. I can't seem to get enough air into my lungs as I inhale.

I'm on the verge of a panic attack when Emmy's voice breaks through to me, her trying to defend me to Ryan and Joanne, and she's trying to explain our situation.

None of them notice the little stick in my hand as I stand back up.

"Emmy," I practically whisper, and my throat feels like it has rocks in it.

Deciding at this moment that I don't care who fathered the baby. She and the baby are mine!

When she doesn't stop her plea with Joanne, willing her to understand, I say her name again.

"Emmy." This time, it comes out loud and booming, filling the hallway.

She spins, looking at me. She catches a glimpse of the stick in my hand, and her hands fly up to her face, covering her nose and mouth in a silent gasp.

"What's that?" Joanne asks, wiping the tears from her cheek and pulling out of Ryan's grip.

She looks at it, then at me, then at Emmy, who's still covering her face.

"Emmy, you're pregnant," I try to ask, yet it comes out more a statement than a question.

She closes the small space between us and reaches for the stick. Handing it over to her, I let my hand brush along hers as she takes it from me.

"I am?" she says looking down at it. "I hadn't read it yet." Her body is now visibly shaking.

I wrap her in my arms, pulling her to me.

"It's okay, Angel." I kiss the top of her head.

"You're pregnant?" Joanne asks in shock.

Emmy nods to her mom, still leaning against my chest; no words coming from her.

Joanne steps closer, opening her arms for Emmy. I hesitantly loosen my hold on her so Joanne can embrace her daughter.

"I'm going to be a grandma." Joanne croaks out. The hurt and pain from a moment ago was replaced with something else.

She hugged Emmy tightly.

Ryan clears his throat uncomfortably.

"*Um*, I don't want to be the one to ask this, but do you know who the father is?"

Emmy's face goes red, and she stiffens at the question.

"It doesn't matter; Emmy is mine, and so the baby will be too."

She turns so fast to look up at me. Tears building in her honey eyes.

"You think this baby could be anyone else but yours?" She pokes my chest as she asks.

I rub a hand up her arm, and she pulls back. "No," she says and swats my hand away.

Turning to look at Ryan.

Fuming mad now. She steps inches from him. "Not that it is any of your business, but Adrian is the only person I have been with in over a year, and he is absolutely the only person who has ever been inside me without a condom."

With that, she stepped back into the office and shut the door, closing us all out. I heard the lock click in place.

I can't help the chuckle that escapes me or the smile that spreads across my face.

I love that fierce crudeness she gets when she's upset; when she's angry, she loses all filters, and I find it frustrating and sexy as hell.

A primal pride fills me with her words too. No one else but me.

Joanne surprises me by coming over and kissing me on the cheek.

"It'll be all right. You two will work it out."

Then, she gives my hand a squeeze.

"Not that I'm happy about the two of you, but I know how my daughter feels about you and what you did for her that night. She told me all about it; she happened to leave out one important thing like your name, but I'll get over it."

She turns to walk back to Ryan, who still hasn't moved since Emmy yelled at him.

"But if you hurt her…" she trails off, leaving it as an open statement.

I nod at her knowingly.

Ryan pulls her into him, kissing her intently.

I look down.

Once he lets her go, he looks back at me.

"We have a lot more to talk about, little brother, but tonight I'm going to let it go. Get some sleep."

"So, I'm not kicked out?"

"Don't press your luck." He scowls.

I don't say anything back because he's right, and I don't need to give him another reason to kick me out, not when I need to be close to Emmy.

Watching as he leads Joanne back up to their own room.

Letting out a heavy breath, I run my hand through my hair.

I have royally fucked this all up.

Walking to the kitchen, I grab a frozen bag of peas from the freezer and press the cold pack to my throbbing cheek.

I have to laugh. Not sure how I was expecting he would react, but a right hook wasn't what I had expected that's for sure.

Ryan had clearly taken to the more paternal protective role than I would have thought possible. I was a little glad for it; she didn't seem to have that growing up.

He didn't need to protect her from me, though; I would protect Emmy and that baby with my life.

I need to find a place for Emmy and the baby; getting my life back is more important than ever now.

I can't even believe she's going to have a baby.

Our baby.

My heart leaps with excitement, fear, and all the emotions at once. I had never thought this would be an option. Now I wanted it more than I could imagine, and I can't wait to see Emmy round with our baby.

Walking back to the office door. I knock lightly.

"Angel, are you still awake?"

No reply.

I don't want to leave her side again. We haven't even talked about us yet.

How is she feeling about this? Shit, does she even want the baby? Questions we will have to talk about in the morning.

Trying the handle, it jiggles; it's still locked. Walking back to the guest room, I grab a blanket and pillow off the bed.

Folding the blanket in half longways and laying it on the floor just outside the office door, I grab the pillow and slip in between the fold, placing the frozen peas back on my cheek. I curl up and drift off.

* * *

A nudge to the shoulder wakes me. Blinking, I look around a little confused. Oh, that's right. I slept on the floor next to the office.

Joanne smiles down at me.

"Would you like some coffee?"

I sit up, stretching my stiff arms out. "Yeah. That would be great. Thanks," I say sleepily.

Joanne offers her hand out to help me stand. I take it, but I use my own body strength to stand.

Leaning down, I grab the now-thawed peas from the floor to place back in the freezer or trash whatever Joanne prefers.

"You can toss those," she says over her shoulder as if she could read my mind.

I follow behind her into the kitchen. The coffee is already brewed; she pours two cups and motions for me to take a seat at the center island.

Sitting next to me, she passes me the steaming cup.

"Cream or sugar?" Joanne offers.

"No thanks; black is fine."

Blowing lightly on the brownish-black liquid before taking a sip.

Mmmhh, not bad. The rich flavor coats my mouth, and the aroma is welcome. I swear, the smell alone helps you wake up.

"I'm going to be frank with you, Adrian," she says, sitting down, her own cup. Her expression is hard, her lips pursed.

"Please do."

"I said as much last night, but I am not fond of the idea of you and my daughter; for Christ sake, you are older than I am."

"Only by a year," I interject.

"I wasn't finished."

"Sorry."

"As I was saying, with that being said, I do know how you two met, and Emmy isn't a child; she's an adult who can make her own choices. Ryan may not be so forgiving, but I'm pretty sure he feels betrayed that you hid it."

"I hate what I did," I add.

She held up a hand in protest. Taking another sip of her coffee then continues.

"All I care about is Emmy and now my grandbaby. If you can't be what they need. then do me a favor and don't try to be because you think it's the right thing to do. Just say goodbye now."

"I'm not going anywhere, Joanne. I know it sounds crazy, but Emmy has my heart; since the second I met her, she became my world."

"I am not one to judge the quickness of your relationship. I get that part. It's not like Ryan and I took things slow."

Her expression lightens and a small smile forms on her face.

"The hard parts about to begin for you, that's going to be proving what you are saying is real to Emmy."

I laugh

"Yeah, I have a lot of things to prove to her."

"She hasn't had it easy; the men in her life always let her down," Joanne adds.

A gruff voice comes from behind us.

"Are we talking to him now?" Ryan walks up, wraps his arms around his wife, and kisses her on the top of the head.

"Morning," I say.

Ryan tilts his head at me. "Nice shiner."

"Want some coffee, love?" Joanne asks

"I can get it, thank you," he says, walking around the island and getting himself a cup.

Emmy

Warm rays of light shine on my face, rubbing my eyes and stretching out my body, I look around the bright office. I must have slept in a bit.

I can hear the hushed voices coming from down the hall. I'm glad it's not more yelling.

I'm still trying to wrap my head around the events of last night. I grab my phone, pull open my notes pad, and add another line.

How to have a one-night stand
Never go home with a stranger from the bar
Never develop feelings for the guy
Never invite him to stay over a second night
Never ever have sex with him a second time
Never get knocked up…

I need a shower. Getting up off the couch, I grab some clothes and my toiletries and head to the bathroom. As I open the office door, I have to step over a pillow and blanket to get out.

Did Adrian sleep out here?

He's such a mystery; I don't know what to do. My mind is at war when it comes to him. My rational side vs. my emotional side.

Shaking my head, I step over and walk to the bathroom. Flipping on the shower to warm up the water.

After brushing my teeth and stripping off the sweats, I climb into the warm stream.

It doesn't take long to wash my hair and body; the warm water feels good, but I know I have to face the day. And I am starving.

I grab the towel off the rack, dry, and put on my jeans, pants that I'm sure won't fit soon, and a black tank top. Then, I run a brush through my long hair, leaving it down to air dry. I dab a little concealer under my still tired looking eyes. Once I give myself a look over in the mirror and am satisfied I don't look like the walking dead, I take in a deep breath.

Here goes nothing; time to face what's to come head on. Time to deal with the mess I've ended up in now. I take one more glance in the mirror, then head to join the others in the kitchen.

* * *

Walking down the aisle of the grocery stores, picking out a few things I would need for my apartment. I have been tired all day, and my body still adjusting to the major time difference between here and Italy.

Pulling out my phone to look at the time, it's just after five p.m., which means it is just past eight a.m. in Italy, perfect time to call Lucy.

The phone only rings twice before she picks up.

"Ciao Cara."
"Hello, dear to you too," I answer with a laugh.
"How was your first day back?" Lucy asks.
"About what I could expect it to be, I guess."
"Did you get to see the sexy Adrian Montgomery?"
"Of course, that is the first thing you want to know."
"Well, I'm living vicariously through you," Lucy says longingly.

I can picture her now sitting at the little table on the balcony of the house we shared, chin in her hand, elbow propped on the table, with the doe eyes she always gets when she talks about anything loving or romantic. Lucy, the endless romantic; she's like a damn Disney character.

"It was late when we got in last night, so I ended up staying over at Mom, and Ryan's; to my surprise, Adrian was also staying there."
"Oh, my gosh!"
"Tell me about it." I sigh. *"I tried to ignore him, but he's just so..."*
"Intense," Lucy provides for me.
"Exactly."
"SOOOO, what happened? Don't leave me hanging."

I look around the semi-crowded store before continuing; no one seems to be paying attention to anything except their own tasks.

Good, I didn't need the world to know my business.

"Well, my relationship with Adrian came up when he got mad about me selling my paintings; Ryan punched him in the face, then he slept on the floor outside the office when I didn't want to talk to him, and thanks for the jinx cuz I am indeed pregnant. Oh, and at a very awkward breakfast this morning, I guess I agreed to see where things could go between us, as long as he's willing to take things slow." I blurted it all out, afraid I wouldn't have the nerve to tell her if I didn't.

"Hold up a minute. Slow down. Start from the beginning."

I spend the next fifteen minutes in the cereal aisle telling Lucy all about what happened last night and this morning. Including how Adrian just wanted to jump into an instant relationship, but I couldn't do it. I wanted to, but I knew we needed to really get to know each other first. He had told me why he sold the house, that he had been going to therapy, working through his past, and how he wanted to make us work.

I agreed to try, but slowly. I made my first Dr. appointment for tomorrow; he was going to be meeting me there, which I was excited for.

We ended our call with a promise to talk more soon; she had to get to class soon. And I was still at the grocery store.

"Scuse me," a little boy says as he's trying to reach around me to grab a box of cereal off the shelf.

Putting my phone in my pocket, I move over.

"Sorry." I smile down at the little boy.

"It otay." He looks up at me and smiles big, holding his box triumphantly.

I'm taken aback. His honey-colored eyes sparkle up at me, and his dusty-colored hair falls a little shaggy around his round face. A face that under the baby fat looks like my father.

I look around the aisle.

On the other end, heading toward us, is another identical little boy running in front of a cart, pushed by a slender man with dusty brown hair, and honey eyes. A man I last saw pumping gas five years ago.

"Dillon, Davis, come on." His voice felt like it echoed through my body.

I'm frozen in place as he gets closer.

The little boys placed the box in the cart. "I don't like that one, Davis," the other little boy says.

"It my favowite," he protested.

"We can only get one," the man says.

The second boy huffs and drops his shoulders a little.

At the same time, the man looks up from the boys, and the cart, for the first time, looks at the girl frozen in front of him. I exhale slowly.

The recognition and realization crosses on his face.

Shaking my head slightly to pull myself together, I look at the little boys; they have to be like four and five or maybe even twins. Then I look back up at him; he's looking at me still.

"Emmy," his voice cracks as he says my name.

"Hi." I don't know what else to say to him.

"Who's that, Daddy?" the other boy asks.

"Dillon, this is Daddy's friend Emmy," he answers.

A part of my heart broke at his words. I don't know what I expected him to say.

"I Davis, I five." The first little boy smiles big at me, holding up his hand to show me his five fingers.

"You're not five yet, Davis." Dillon chastises his brother. "My name's Dillon." He smiles a little skeptical at me.

"Nice to meet you boys." I smile at the little boys who have my eyes. "How old are you, Dillon?" I bend down so I'm closer to his height.

"Seven."

He had a kid already the last time I saw him. I wonder if he was in the car at the station, and I bet the lady was pregnant with the younger one. How could he do that to them and to me? Feelings of not being good enough for him threaten to take over my mind.

"I gotta go. Nice to see you." I say, grabbing my cart and walking the other direction.

Too many emotions hitting me all at once. I just needed to get away.

"She pretty, Daddy," Davis says as I'm walking away.

"Yeah, she is, buddy; let's go get some cupcakes for tomorrow."

My heart was beating so fast by the time I made it to my car, I hurried through self-checkout.

I don't know what I expected or why I thought he would ever tell me if he had a new family, but that didn't stop it from hurting.

I pushed the unlock and trunk pop on the key fob. Breathing in and out a few times to slow my heart rate, light tears slip down my face.

I load my bags then shut the trunk and try to hold back the wave of nausea.

"Are you okay?"

"Fine." I look over and see my father standing next to me, and the boys are climbing into the backseat of the car in the parking spot next to mine.

He looks at me, a little worried. He reaches out like he's going to pat me on the arm. I stand up, raising my hand in front of me.

"I'm fine. Thanks."

His hand drops to his side.

"I'm sorry," he says, guilt in his eyes.

"It's not you; I'm just pregnant." Only a half lie.

His eyes go wide.

"Guess you aren't a little girl anymore."

"I haven't been for a long time," I say flatly.

"Well, it looks like you're doing just fine," he says condescending and gestures to the cresting.

"I am."

Giving him a good look-over, something I didn't do in the store because I was in shock. I notice his once handsome features are a little sunken in, his slender build even more skin and bones. The car he's driving is an old model with rust spots. It's in rough shape, worse than my old car, and I'm not even sure it's safe to drive.

Then I look at the two little boys in the back seat. They seem happy and healthy, but the youngest still has baby fat. The older one, although a bit on the smaller side, still looks healthy, just short and slender. He looks like my father used to in the pictures I've seen.

Their clothes were worn but seemed to be washed.

"Where have you been?" I ask.

He looks at me, and for a minute, I wonder if he's going to answer or not. His face falls a little, losing the judging look from a minute ago.

"Their mother, Tina, and I moved to California. When I had gotten my life together, I did reach out to your mom; I did want to see you." He pauses, then adds, "Tina knew about you; she went to school with us, but then she got pregnant with our first, and she wanted it to be just our family. We tried to stay around here for a while, but after seeing you at the gas station that day, Tina was pregnant with Davis. We decided to move; she said it was too much to see you around."

"Why are you back?"

"Tina died a few months ago; her sister lives here still, and I was hoping she could help me with the boys."

"I'm so sorry," I say.

"None of that." He waves me off. "It was good to see you," he adds, giving me a small smile.

"Good to see you too, James."

He turns away from me, glancing back over his shoulder once, then gets in his car.

Adrian

It had been torture to let Emmy leave to go back to her apartment, but I promised her I'd try slow, even though I knew what I wanted and it was a life with her.

I didn't want to push her away. Joanne was right; I was going to have to work for it.

Sitting with my laptop open on my desk in the back office of Tipsy Roots, my bar.

I sip on a scotch.

I had a few business things to take care of; I have already called and checked in with my manager at the bar in Oregon.

Now I was here checking in with Anthony before heading out for the evening.

"You're a lucky bastard." Anthony walking into the office.

"Don't I know it?"

"Any luck with the painting yet?" he asks.

This morning I had given a call to the auction site Emmy used to sell her work on; they wouldn't give me any information about the purchaser, so I enlisted Anthony's help on this task too.

It only took him an hour to hack their purchase information and get me the name, phone number, email, and home address of the person who bought the shibari piece.

"Not yet, I left a message and sent an email. I haven't had a reply yet."

"I don't blame you for wanting that back."

Anthony had seen the images of the painting when he was finding the info for me.

"No kidding. I can't believe she sold it."

"It's a damn good resemblance." He winks at me.

"Do you want an ass kicking?"

"Now, now," he teases.

"You don't get to admire my girl that way. Got it."

"Got it, boss. Her friend is more my type anyway."

"Get your ass back behind the bar before I replace you permanently." I huff at him.

Anthony had taken a couple weeks off earlier in the month for some personal stuff, and while he was out, one of our part-time guys had filled in for him. He did a good job, but Anthony knows damn well there is no replacing him.

"Don't threaten me with a good time." He laughs and heads out toward the bar.

After another thirty minutes of focusing on my work, it's getting harder to drown out all the noises coming from the bar. The bar is getting busier the later it gets. There's quite a few patrons here for a Thursday night.

That's great for my pocket—not so much for concentration, though.

The growing glorification of the MC world in some TV shows had more young girls coming in anytime Anthony had his bike parked outside, and some of his biker friends frequented the bar during the week as well.

Anthony no longer belonged to a charter, but he had made good with the local chapter, so we didn't have any issues here.

The guys who frequented were all decent guys, so I didn't mind them hanging around as long as their club business didn't interfere with my bar business.

Closing the laptop, I decide to call it a night.

I want to swing over and check on Emmy before I head back to Ryans.

Pulling out my phone, I decide to text her first, make sure she's home and okay with me stopping over. I haven't seen her since breakfast and that feels like forever ago.

Me: Hey Angel, you home?
Angel: I am
Me: I'm just finishing up some work and wanted to stop by if that's okay with you.

The little dots indicating she's writing appear and disappear for a minute before she finally replies.

Angel: That's fine.
Me: Need anything?
Angel: No, all good.
Me: See you soon.

I place my phone back in my pocket. Place my laptop in the bag, I close the office door, and head to the bar to let Anthony know I'm bouncing and make sure he doesn't need anything, or need me to call in anyone to help him out tonight since it's a bit busier than usual.

"I'm out of here," I shout to Anthony.

He waves and gives me a nod.

"You good?" I ask before walking away.

"All good, boss. Give Emmy a snuggle for me." He winks.

I shake my head at him; if I didn't know him like I do, I'd kick his ass. Hell, I still might.

As I'm turning to go, a scrawny guy bumps into my arm. Grabbing ahold of me so he doesn't fall from the force of the impact.

Removing his hands from my arm, I straighten him up.

"You good?" I look down at the man.

His shaggy hair fell forward, covering most of his face.

"A-all g-ood." He slurs.

Clearly intoxicated.

I motion to Anthony. He quickly makes his way around the bar and to my side.

"Find this man a ride home."

"Sure thing."

Stepping aside, handing off the guy to Anthony. He pulls his arm away, pushing aside his hair.

"Heyy, man, y-you can't cut me off."

"I just did," I say, turning back to look at him.

His eyes are glossy; he's more than drunk; he's high on something. Even with the dim lighting and glossy eyes, his features look familiar, but I can't place it. His pupils are dilated; it's hard to see in the lighting what their true color is, and his face is sunken in, probably from lack of nutrition and regular drug use.

"Can you handle this?" I ask Anthony.

"Yeah, I'll have Denver help me out while we wait on a cab."

Anthony calls over one of his biker friends.

"Thanks guys."

"Look, man, Anthony and Denver here are going to get you a burger and a ride home. Sober up and take care of yourself."

"I d-donttt need your charity."

"Not a charity man, just lookin' out." I pat him on the back and walk away, I know he won't be going anywhere until Anthony sticks him in the back of the cab himself.

* * *

I felt like a giddy teenager headed over to his crush's house as I pulled into Emmy's apartment complex.

I grab the flowers I stopped for on the way here off the passenger seat and lock the car door.

Knocking on the door, waiting for her to answer, I look around the complex; the sun has gone down, and I notice there isn't the greatest lighting from the parking lot to the buildings. It's not the worst place out here but I don't like her living here, alone either. The windows aren't thick, and neither is the front door. Someone could easily break into a place like this.

When she answers, I'm still looking around. The squeak of the door opening turns my attention to her.

I smile down at her; she's standing in the doorway in gray leggings and a maroon off-shoulder oversized shirt, her hair hangs in natural waves down her back and shoulders.

"Hey there, gorgeous."

Her cheeks turn that perfect pink shade that I love seeing on them.

"Hey you." She smiles back. Her eyes light up when she sees the bundle of flowers.

"Are those for me?"

She moves aside so I can enter the apartment. I walk a small distance into the room, closing the door behind me.

"Of course, Angel."

I hand her the bouquet; it's made up of sunflowers, pink lilies, and white snapdragons.

"They are so pretty. Thank you."

"They reminded me of you."

She brings the bouquet to her nose and inhales deeply.

"They smell amazing too."

Walking to the little kitchen, she grabs a vase from the cabinet under the sink.

Now that I'm here, I don't quite know what to do or how to act. I would normally just tell or show her what I want, but we are treading on new territory here. I don't know how to be a boyfriend anymore; Sarah was so long ago, and I clearly fucked up that relationship.

Also, the last time I was standing here wasn't the best point in my life, and I had a lot to make up for.

"Come on in."

I follow Emmy to the couch. She takes a seat and pulls her feet up, crossing them in front of her.

I take a seat on the other side of the couch, nervously running a hand through my hair.

"How was your day?" I ask casually.

"It was a bit weird, honestly," she says, giving me a small shrug, before leaning over to the coffee table, she grabs a cup and sips on whatever she's drinking. Tea, I think.

"Everything okay?"

"Yeah, nothing's wrong, just stressed."

"Come here." I reach for her.

Emmy wastes no time as she sets her cup down and crawls toward me. I pull her into my lap, her back to my front. She lays her head back against my chest and exhales a heavy breath. I kiss the top of her head and just hold her against me.

"Thank you," she whispers.

"Anytime, Angel."

She shifts in my lap, so she is now straddling my lap. Wrapping her arms around my neck. Since we are on tricky ground at the moment, I let her lead, not taking anything she doesn't want to give.

I gently rub a hand up and down her back over her sweater.

She lays her head on my shoulder.

"I'm so sorry, Angel; I've missed you so much," I whisper against her ear.

"Missed you too." She sighs. "I didn't want to miss you."

My heart hurts at her words. I fucked up royally that day.

Emmy

Sitting on Adrian's lap feels like home; his soft strokes down my back relax me.

I snuggle into his neck; his signature scent fills my nostrils as I take in a deep breath.

My body responds with need. It's like I have been drowning, and he is my life preserver.

I'm still terrified he is going to hurt me, but right now I don't care.

Lacing my fingers in his hair, I place soft kisses to his neck, trailing up to his ear, and I suck in his earlobe.

He sucks in a breath. I can feel him harden, pressed beneath my ass.

One hand slips under the hem of my sweater, his touch burning delicious trails of fire up my spine.

Leaning back, I look in his eyes; they are filled with lust and desire.

"Make me forget why this isn't a good idea," I say before crushing my lips to his.

His arms squeeze me to him, and I rock on his lap, grinding onto his cock.

I moan into his mouth as he trails his hands up my sides. Our kiss, hot and hard, a tangle of tongues.

Adrian pulls away first, both of us out of breath.

"So damn beautiful." He groans out.

"Please, Adrain, I need you," I practically beg.

Adrian stands with me in his arms still, wrapping my legs around his waist. I cling to his hard body, needing the feel of him. He walks us to my bedroom, kicking the door closed behind him.

We are cloaked in darkness. Painfully slow, he walks to my bed, laying me down onto the mattress. I release my grip from around him.

Cupping my face with his hands, he pulls me into another kiss before stepping back.

My heart rate picks up, pounding with a rush of excitement, anticipating what's to come.

My eyes adjust to the dark. I look up at him, staring down at me.

"I have dreamed of having you again, Angel."

His voice is deep and husky, almost pained.

"I'm right here."

I slowly pull off my sweater and toss it to the side. I love how his eyes follow the movements of my hands. I reach behind me and unclip my bra, adding it to the pile.

He lets out a low growl, closing the distance from where he was standing to the bed. Climbing up on his hands and knees, he stalks over top of me, grabbing my hands in one of his and lifting them above my head, gripping them so I can't touch him, pressed firmly into the mattress. Then his mouth captures a breast, circling his tongue on the peak as he gently bites down on the nipple. His free hand works my other breast, pinching the slight pressure, reminding me of the clamps he used on me before.

Wet heat pools between my thighs. I moan, bucking up.

"You're going to be a good girl if I release your hands."

"Yes," I reply breathless.

Adrain lets go of my wrists.

"Grip the blanket, Angel."

I do as he asks, fisting the blanket at my sides.

He leans down whispering into the shell of my ear.

"That's a good girl."

God, the way he says that sends chills through my whole body.

He blows warm breath along my jaw, followed by soft kisses. He does this all the way down my body until he's at the waist band of my leggings.

My body is so worked up, I'm gripping the blanket so tight.

He lays one more kiss on my navel, then grips my leggings and pulls them down my legs. I kick my feet, helping him get them all the way off. I'm left lying on the bed, breathing heavily in nothing. As I hadn't bothered to wear anything under my leggings.

"Angel."

I spread wide, inviting him in.

Adrian grabs hold of my leg, kissing from my foot all the way up until he's placing kisses on my inner thigh.

I squirm, wanting more, needing more—this is fucking torture.

"Please," I whimper.

I am rewarded when he parts my folds and slips a finger into me.

"Yes." I moan.

He chuckles and adds a second finger, pumping them deliciously in and out of my wet pussy.

Leaning down, he sucks my clit into his mouth as he works me with his fingers. Rotating his tongue, across my clit with soft licks, flicks, and sucks.

Oh god, this is exactly what I needed. He makes me feel so good. Like no one else could. I don't ever want it to stop. He curls his fingers inside me, hitting that spot that sends a jolt through me. As my climax nears, I squeeze his fingers.

I'm panting, and sweat is dripping down my skin with his sweet torture. I want to reach down and grip his hair.

"That's it, baby, cum for me." He breathes against my sensitive skin, and I lose control as a wave of ecstasy crashes over me.

Shaking from the intensity of my orgasm, breathing heavily, I throw my head back as I ride out my release.

He slips his fingers from me, bringing them to his mouth and sucking them clean.

"Best damn thing I've ever tasted."

Adrian

I could listen to her pants and moans all night.

I'm so fucking hard, my cock is ready to burst through my pants.

I need to be inside her so fucking bad.

I smile down at her as her eyes close.

"I'm not done with you yet, Angel."

Stepping off the bed, I strip off my clothes. Emmy sits up in the bed, eyes going wide. As I free my cock from its restraint, it bobs out, hard and heavy.

I almost blow my load when she licks her lips.

"I'm not going to last long if you keep looking at me like that."

I stalk back to the bed.

Climbing on, I lay next to her.

"Come here, baby, I want to watch you ride me."

Without hesitation, she throws one leg over me, kneeling above me, grabbing hold of my shaft and places it at her entrance.

She pauses before sinking down.

"Have you..." Her voice came out shaky and low. "Have you been with someone else?"

Sitting up, I caress a hand along her cheek.

"No. It's only you for me, Emmy."

She leans into my palm and takes in a soft breath. Stroking up and down my length, she re-positions herself. Clasping around her waist, helping her as she slides down, taking my cock into her perfect pussy.

I grunt as she moans, and it's like music to my ears.

She doesn't move for a minute as she lets herself adjust to me.

I release her waist as she places her hands on my chest and pushes me back into the mattress. Pulling her down with me, I grip the back of her neck and kiss her with all the need I have been feeling since she has been gone.

Emmy begins rocking in a slow rhythm, sliding up and down my cock. Before I know it, she's breaking away from the kiss, pressing her hands firmly into my chest, her head pulled back, and her breast bouncing up and down as she speeds her movements, taking me deeper and harder. I thrust my hips to meet her pace. Caressing her thighs, sides, back—any part of her I can get my hands on. I love her small curves. I love her.

It's not long before I feel my balls tighten, ready to explode.

"I'm so close, baby. Cum with me." I grip her nipples, rubbing them both between my thumb and forefinger that does the trick to push her further toward her own release.

"Yes, yes." She pants as she slams back her wet pussy so far down my cock it hurts, in the best way.

Thrusting up, I cum as her walls tighten and milk me, releasing hot, thick cum deep inside her.

I pull her down so she's lying flat across my chest as we both steady our racing hearts.

Kissing the top of her head, she hums in pure bliss, trailing little circles in the light hair that covers my toned chest.

* * *

We must have drifted off to sleep, because the next thing I'm aware of is my phone blaring with a call from the pocket of my jeans, laying on the floor.

I unfold Emmy from my chest, trying not to wake her as I slip out from under her to get the phone.

She rustles and groans.

"*Shh, shh,* it's okay, Angel." I kiss her cheek.

Grabbing the phone, I look at the screen and see Anthony's name flashing on the screen.

I swipe to answer the call and step quietly into the hall.

"There better be a damn good reason you're calling me," I say gruffly pulling the phone from my ear and glancing at the time. *"At two in the morning,"* I add.

"Boss, we have a problem."

Fucking great. I glance back through the door and rub my hand through my hair.

"What is it?"

"I was closing up and noticed there was still a car in the parking lot on the far end. At first, I didn't think anything of it because it's not like people don't leave cars here."

"Would you get to the point?" I say with irritation. I'm standing naked in the hall and not sleeping next to my girl.

"Ugh, yeah, sorry, boss. Anyway, as I was getting ready to head out for a bit when I had a feeling I needed to check on that car, and well, when I drove past it, I noticed there were people sleeping in it."

"That's fine; I'd rather them sleep it off in the parking lot than drive if they are intoxicated. You didn't need to call me for this."

"That's not the problem… the problem is that it's just two little kids."

"Fuck, and no one else is left around?"

"No, boss. What do you want me to do?"

"I'll be there in a minute; hold tight," I say, then hang up.

When I walk back into the room, Emmy is sitting up in bed.

"What's wrong?"

"I gotta deal with an issue at the bar. You get some sleep."

"Everything okay?"

I walk over and give her a kiss after I'm done pulling on my clothes.

"Nothing you need to worry about, Angel. Someone just left their two little kids in the parking lot, and I need to go sort it out, make sure they are okay."

"OH, my gosh." She gasps, scooting out of bed. She hurriedly pulls on her leggings and sweatshirt from earlier.

"I'm going with you."

"I'd rather you stay and get some rest," I say and grab her shoulders.

"No, I'm going with you," she says with a strange look on her face, almost panicked.

I don't argue with her; I just grab her hand and head out the apartment with her.

"Okay, Angel."

I don't know why she is panicking, but I can feel her turmoil.

Once we are in the car and heading toward the bar. I look over at her; she's biting on her bottom lip in deep thought, something clearly bothering her.

"You want to tell me what has you all worked up?"

She looks at me, and I notice tears in her eyes that are threatening to spill over.

I place a hand on her thigh. "What is it?"

"Remember, earlier, I told you I had a weird day?"

"Yeah?" I ask inquiringly.

"I ran into my dad when I was at the store earlier; he had two little boys with him, my brothers."

Brothers? I didn't know she had brothers; I was pretty sure Ryan or Joanne never mentioned other kids.

"And you think that the kids in my parking lot are them?"

"I have a bad feeling they are; there was something kind of off about James, my dad, when I saw him."

Her saying that makes me think back to earlier in the evening when that guy bumped into me at the bar. It couldn't have been him; I hoped it wasn't. That man from the bar was not in a good place.

"We'll be there in a minute and figure this out."

"Thank you," she says placing her hand over mine.

Pulling into the lot, I drive around to the far side, where I spot Anthony leaning against his bike next to a rundown car.

Parking I get out, walking around, and opening the door for Emmy. Helping her out of the car. Anthony straightens and walks toward us.

"Sorry to wake you, boss. I didn't want to call the cops if we didn't have to."

"It's okay. I'm glad you called; it may be even more complicated than we thought." I shrug.

Emmy's a little shaky next to me. "It's his car."

"Who's car?" Anthony asks.

"James, Emmy's dad," I answer for her.

"Are they in there?" she asks, looking from the car to Anthony; she hasn't made a move to walk closer and peek in herself.

He nods his head. "Sleeping the whole time."

"The guy from earlier, did you happen to know where the cab took him?"

"Shit, really. Him." He looks at Emmy and back at me.

I shake my head in acknowledgement.

"He refused the burger and coffee I offered him and tried to start shit with Denver's group. He was spout'n all kinds of nonsense. He couldn't give us an address and was clearly high on something, so when the cab came, we sent him to Bruno's so hopefully he could sober up."

"Bruno's?" Emmy asks.

"Bruno is a buddy of mine who runs a rehab center," he answers. "Sorry, *em*, I didn't know."

"It's okay; I didn't either; I didn't even know he was around or that I had little brothers until earlier today. That's probably where he needs to be anyway."

"What do you want to do about the kids, Angel?"

She lets go of my hand for the first time since we got here and walks over to the car.

Trying the back-door handle, it's not locked, and she opens it slowly. Walking up behind her, I see the two young boys curled on the back seat together.

How could anyone leave their kids in a car while they went to a bar? It makes me want to kick the shit out of James.

"We should wake them and see if they can tell us where their aunt lives. James told me earlier that they were here to stay with their mom's sister."

She reaches in and rubs the arm of the oldest boy.

"Dillon, honey."

The boy stretches in the small space, blinking, then opening his eyes. He bolts up in surprise and confusion.

"It's okay, Dillon. I'm not going to hurt you. I just need to ask you a few questions."

He scoots forward on the seat closer to the open door, blocking his little brother from view.

"Do you remember me from earlier?" she asks calmly.

He blinks at her a few times, rubbing his eyes with his little hands.

"Yeah, Emmy, dad's friend."

Emmy crouches down next to him and smiles.

"That's right."

"Where's my dad?" the little boy asks.

She looks over her shoulder at me questioningly.

"I'll make a phone call." I step a few feet away from them and back to Anthony, who is already on the phone, hopefully with Bruno, so we can find out the condition of James.

Emmy

Adrian walked over to Anthony, and I can hear them on the phone, so I turn my attention back to Dillon.

"We are going to find out and make sure he's okay." I try to keep my voice calm and soft, even though on the inside I'm anything but.

I have had all kinds of emotions since running into him today, and now I'm just pissed off. How could he do this to these boys?

"I'm sorry I woke you, but I wanted to get you somewhere safe."

Dillon looks around, confused.

"We're safe," he says and puffs up like I insulted him.

"Do you know where your aunt lives?"

He shakes his head. But doesn't answer.

"Emmwy?" a sleepy little voice asks from behind Dillon.

He peeks his head around his brother's shoulder, and I smile at him.

"Hi, Davis."

Dillon grabs his little brother and holds onto him protectively.

"Just trying to find you boys a bed to sleep in."

His eyes go wide. "A bed? We don't have a bed."

"Davis, be quiet. Remember what Dad said?"

"Sorry, Dil."

"It's okay, boys; I'm a friend, remember. You can talk to me."

Dillon looks behind me, so I look to where he's looking.

"You don't have to worry about them either, they are my friends and we all just want to help you," I say and gesture to the guys.

"Do you know how far away your aunt's house is from the grocery store we were at?"

"We don't have an aunt. That's something Dad told us to say if anyone ever asks where we are staying," Dillon answers.

Oh, no, my heart sinks, I hope they haven't been living out of this car. I am sure I know the answer before I even ask the question.

"Is the car where you always stay?"

"Ya, but we get to go to the park for my birthday," he says excitedly, almost jumping out of Dillon's arms. "You can come, can ya, can ya?"

"Maybe, buddy, let's figure out a better place to sleep tonight first, okay?"

"Okay," he says.

"Dillon, how long have you been staying in the car?"

"Since Mom," he says sadly.

"How long have you been around here?"

He thinks for a minute. Then shrugs. "Not long."

I stand up and offer my hand to the boys.

"Come with me; you can stay with me tonight."

Davis jumps up excitedly and grabs my hand. Dillon looks back at the car, then, decides to trust me and follows me toward Adrian and Anthony, who are only a few feet away next to his car.

I help the boys get into the back of the car.

"Buckle up. We will be on our way soon," I say, giving the boys a soft smile.

Closing the car door and turning back to Anthony and Adrian. Adrian holds out an arm for me, and I gladly walk into his embrace. He pulls me tight to his chest, kissing me softly on my head.

"What do you want to do, Angel?" he asks.

"I don't know. They need a safe place to sleep, so for now, can we just take them home?"

"Of course." Adrian gives me a reassuring squeeze.

"I'll follow up with Bruno and let you know," Anthony says, then pats Adrian on the shoulder.

Adrian nods a thanks and walks me back to the passenger side of his car, opening the door and helping me in before walking to the driver side.

The rumble of Anthony's motorcycle fills the quiet night as he takes off out of the parking lot.

Inhale and let out a deep breath. Just breathe, I tell myself, glancing back at the two little boys in the backseat. Davis is already slumped into Dillon.

* * *

Both boys had crashed on the short drive over, and I couldn't bear to wake them up again. I couldn't help the smile across my face as I watched Adrain carry in the boys one by one and place them in Lucy's bed. He was so gentle with them; they didn't even stir when he pulled them into his big arms.

It makes me think about the little one growing inside of me, and how he will be as a dad.

Tucking the blanket up around them and flipping the light on the nightstand to the dimmest setting, taking one last look at their little faces, I leave the door cracked slightly and join Adrian in the front room.

"I'm sorry," I say, unsure what else to say, this just adds to all the crap we have to work through already.

"Me too, Angel. So fucking sorry."

And I know he's not just talking about tonight.

I lean up on my tip toes and kiss his cheek.

Grabbing hold of my wrist, he brings my hand to his mouth and kisses my knuckles.

"You should probably get some sleep. It's almost three a.m.," he says.

"I'll be okay," I say, and as if my body is betraying me, I try to hide a yawn.

He chuckles.

"We have a big day ahead, lots to figure out still. You get some sleep, and I'll work on finding out what we need to do for the boys."

"I don't want them going back to him," I say yawning again. Even though I hardly know them, I feel very protective of them. There is no way I'm letting them go back to a drug addict who leaves them alone in a car.

"I know, Angel; we'll figure it all out later."

"I don't want to leave you to do this on your own," I argue. After a few more attempts to get me to go to bed, Adrian caves and compromises with sitting on the coach, me curled up with my head on his lap as he rotates from typing on his phone and making phone calls.

He strokes my hair from my face absentmindedly, and I love it. I love how it calms the raging storm of emotions running through me over seeing my dad again and then realizing what type of person he really is or still is. I don't really know what to do with all that's going on in my life right now. Let's not forget the discovery of having two little brothers and finding out I'm pregnant added onto all this stress. It's just all so much in such a short time.

Part of me is glad Adrian is here and wanting to help me with this. It gives me hope—hope that he can be who I imagine him to be—a man that wants to be in my life for me, not the completely broken man I first met and fell for in the bar.

It feels like a lifetime ago that I met him, even though it's only been three months. I don't know how it's possible to have such strong feelings for someone in such a short time, but I have known from that first day I was going to love this man.

I just hope I'm not the one who is too broken for us to work now.

The long ago fears of abandonment and not feeling worthy flood me unwillingly.

The only thing I am certain of for sure at this moment is that. "I'm in love with Adrian." My eyes catch one last glimpse of his beautiful face before closing, as I drift in and out of consciousness and the exhaustion takes over completely.

Adrian

I am beyond angry; the more I dig into James Johnson, Emmy's biological father, the worse it gets.

I've been looking into what James had told Emmy about where and what he had been up two since she saw him last.

It wasn't too hard to track his steps. It seemed like they were doing good in California. He had a job, his kids were in school and preschool, and from the outside, it looked like things were good for them. That was until his wife died six months ago, the kids got pulled out of school, he stopped going to work, and he racked up a few possession of narcotic charges in California.

Part of me couldn't blame the man for losing it; grief did crazy things to people. I knew that firsthand. But the other part was pissed. Had I had kids, no matter what happened with Sarah, those kids would have come first; they would have been reason enough to fight for sanity and sobriety.

But he didn't do shit to protect his kids, and that started before he had a family with Tina; he had left Joanne and Emmy to fend for themselves back when she was little and never checked to make sure she was okay.

Now he was doing the same thing, or worse, with the boys, choosing drugs over their safety. It made my blood boil. How anyone could leave their kids like that?

I guess I'm just glad he didn't just dump the kids somewhere, and for the most part, they seemed to be taken care of.

None of it made sense to me. Why choose to keep the kids, and where was child protective services? Why had no one looked out for these poor babies?

Not to mention the pain I know he's caused Emmy by not being in her life and finding out about her brothers like this. Plus the pain and turmoil he's causing the boys now.

I don't think she will even admit to herself how his choices have affected her.

"What do you mean?" I ask Anthony, as he tells me they don't know where James is.

"Not sure, boss, but he isn't here," he says on the other end of the line.

I stroke Emmy's hair; it's splayed across my lap. Her being here with me is the only thing keeping my anger inside. I have to smile as I watch her fight the sleep; her eyes flutter open and close.

I don't know how she wrapped herself around my heart so fast, but damn if I wouldn't do anything in my power to make this girl happy. She mumbles as she drifts in and out. I think it's adorable.

"We need to find him. Are you going home to the bar tonight?" I ask.

"Yes, boss, I was going to go back there after checking in with Bruno."

"Good, watch his car; see if he comes back for it."

I try to keep the frustration out of my voice. Anthony has done more than I could ask of him to help me out; it's not his fault we are in this mess.

A soft, barely audible mumble escapes Emmy. "I'm in love with Adrian." I freeze, looking down at her. Her big eyes look back at me with a small smile on her face before her eyes shut and she's out again.

I can't even be sure that's what she really said, but damn if the thought of it doesn't make my heart squeeze.

"Adrian?" Anthony asks, as if I missed something he said.

"Sorry. Distracted," I say.

"Get some rest, boss; we will work it all out."

"Yeah, I probably should." I sigh. "Thanks, man. I owe you a lot."

"Nah, it's nothing," he says before disconnecting the call.

Setting my phone down, I carefully slide out from under Emmy; I walk back to the spare room in her tiny apartment, looking in on the two little boys that look so much like her. My heart hurts for them; they shouldn't have to worry where they are going to sleep if their dad is coming back for them.

They should be happy and carefree. I don't know what Emmy wants to tell them, or what her plan is yet, but I will help her in whatever she decides, and I will make sure these boys get to live the life they deserve no matter what.

I run a hand through my hair and breathe out a steading breath, the stress of all this is a lot.

Deciding this is a little more that the two of us are going to be able to handle on our own, I send off a text to Ryan, letting him know what's going on.

Knowing there isn't much more I can do tonight, I grab Emmy from the couch and tuck her into her bed, stripping down and climbing in next to her. I pull her into me, she curls up, and I wrap my body protectively around her, inhaling her florally sweet scent in and let the darkness take me under.

* * *

The sounds drifting in through the open bedroom door have me sturing, and I lean over and notice Emmy isn't in bed next to me. Sitting up, I stretch and find my clothes from yesterday. Pulling on my pants, I walk out to join the chatter.

Emmy is in the kitchen, while Dillon and Davis are seated on the two bar stools, eating pancakes and drinking orange juice.

She looks over her shoulder at me as she's flipping another pancake and smiles.

"Morning," I say.

She smiles back at me, her eyes brighter than they were yesterday.

"Mister man, mister man!" the younger of the boys, Davis, calls excitedly to get my attention.

"Good morning, little man." I can't help but smile at his chubby little face, and bright honey eyes, and light brown hair. He's adorable.

"I not little anymore; it's my birthday!" he replies with all the enthusiasm of a kid in a candy store.

The older boy rolls his eyes and picks at his plate.

"Well then, happy birthday." I chuckle.

"Are you hungry?" Emmy asks, coming up next to me with a plate full of pancakes.

I can't help it. I reach out, taking the plate from her, setting it on the countertop, and pulling her into me, kissing her on the cheek.

Whispering in her ear, "Hungry for another taste of you."

Her cheeks flush the prettiest pink, and she giggles.

She pushes me away with a grin on her face and shakes her head. "Go put a shirt on."

Laughing I do as she asks and walk back to the bedroom to retrieve a shirt.

It seems so natural to be with her and around her like this.

We all eat together while Davis rambled on about all the things he wants to do today and how his dad promised they would go to the park.

Now they are watching cartoons while Emmy cleans up.

Sitting in the chair on my phone following up with everyone on the situation.

I haven't told Emmy yet that James is MIA.

He didn't go back to the car last night; Anthony had let me know this morning there was no sign of him. I also hadn't had time to tell her that Ryan and Joanne were on their way over to come meet the boys, and take them so we could go to Emmy's Dr. appointment.

Something I don't think she had thought about with all that's going on. The past seventy-two hours have been a lot.

A knock on the door has Emmy jumping, dropping a dish in the sink.

"It's all right," I say, standing and heading to answer the door.

I hate that the tension is back in Emmy's face; she had seemed less on edge this morning. Now that worried, stressed look was back.

Ryan and Joanne enter the apartment carrying bags of stuff with them.

"Good morning." We both greet each other.

Emmy leaves her dishes in the sink, wipes her hands on a cloth, and walks over, giving her mom a quick hug. I can see the tears she's holding back as she does.

"Why are you here?" Emmy asks.

Joanne nods toward the boys. "Adrian gave us a heads up."

She lets go of her mom and walks her toward the boys.

Ryan pats me on the back. I guess he's gotten past being angry with me.

"Quite the mess you're in," he says, no judgment in his tone.

"It appears so," I acknowledge, we turn our attention to the girls.

Emmy is talking to the boys, introducing them to her mom. Davis is as excited as he always seems to be. While Dillon is quiet and withdrawn, studying the situation.

I think that kid understands more going on around him than most probably think.

"Have you found their father yet?" Ryan asks.

"Not yet."

"Kind of weird; he would just disappear like that, not even go back to check on the boys." Ryan contemplates.

"Drugs make people do stupid things." I shrug.

"It's the little one's birthday; we should try and make it as normal as possible for him, even though he doesn't know us and the one person he does know is missing," I tell Ryan.

He agrees.

"Joanne also brought them some new clothes; she insisted when I told her what was going on."

"This can't be easy for her," I add.

"I think her only concern is for Emmy and those little boys. She lived with the disappointment and lies from him for a long time, but this is new to them."

Emmy

After introducing the boys to Ryan and my mom, sending them off to get dressed in their new clothes. We made plans to meet them at the park after my appointment, the one I had spaced out completely.

I reluctantly left the kids with them; I can't even imagine all that's going through their little minds. They are with complete strangers, and even though I'm a stranger to them too, I feel a protective bond over them. I wish I had known them sooner and been able to be there to help in some way.

I know what it's like to feel abandoned, and I want to save my brothers from that as much as possible.

A soft yet firm grip on my thigh pulls me from my thoughts.

"It's going to be okay," Adrian says to me.

"I know," I say trying to keep the nervousness out of my voice.

"You're twitching, Angel." That's when I realized the nervous bouncing of my leg up and down.

"Oh, sorry, a lot is running through my mind."

I'm thankful he doesn't press more. He just nods, leaving his hand on my thigh, and returns his attention to his phone.

The *tick tick* of the clock hanging above the reception desk isn't helping my nerves. As I look around the tiny waiting room, there are magazines on the table in front of me, a young couple in the far corner smiling and laughing with each other, and a single women who is very pregnant sitting reading one of the provided magazines.

I wonder what their lives are like—do they have all kinds of crazy shit going on in their lives too?

"Johnson," a bubbly blonde girl calls from a side door.

Adrian stands, pocketing his phone, and offers me a hand. I wipe my sweaty palms on my yoga pants, taking his outstretched hand.

We follow the bubbly nurse into an exam room. She asks me a bunch of questions, then has me go pee in a cup and takes some blood. Then I undress and wait on the cold table. All while Adrian sits in an uncomfortable-looking chair and waits, paying attention to all the questions the nurse asks. Helping me with my gown, he kisses my forehead and takes my hand.

The doctor knocks and walks in, almost at the same time. Thank the heavens, I was already sitting back down. Although I guess it's not going to matter soon, he will be examining all my delicate parts.

"Good afternoon. I'm Dr. Taylor."

Adrian scowls as a very good-looking doctor enters the room.

I want to laugh, but I can't. I love the possessiveness. I grip his hand in a reassuring gesture.

Dr. Taylor looks over the notes from the nurse. Sitting on a swivel stool, he rolls over to me.

"The urine sample came back positive, but we are also running a blood test, and I'm going to do a little exam."

"Okay," I say both excited and nervous.

Adrian holds my hand the entire exam; if he was uncomfortable or nervous by any of it, he didn't let on.

When we finally get to the part where we get to see the baby, I'm nervous.

"Because it's early in the pregnancy, we use the internal wand to do the ultrasound."

The initial intrusion of the wand was uncomfortable, but any fear, any nervousness I was feeling wipes away as I watched the monitor.

A black and gray grainy image filled the screen. In the center of a dark misshapen bubble was another gray shape; it was like a kidney bean with little stubby arms and legs. Didn't quite look like what I picture a baby to look like, but there it was forming.

"Everything is looking good," Dr. Taylor says as he takes some measurements on the screen and snaps some still shots.

"That's our baby." Adrian chokes out, tears slipping down his face.

"It sure is, measuring about eight weeks along with a due date of May 30," Dr. Taylor says.

I can't believe it; the screen blurs behind the tears in my eyes.

Dr. Taylor finishes his exam, prints out a sonogram photo of our little bean, and exits the room for me to get dressed.

It's like I'm in a daze after seeing the baby on the screen. It's real—so very real.

I wipe up the rest of the jelly, and Adrian helps me get dressed. We see the nurse and schedule our next appointment.

We are in the car, driving toward the park, before I gain my mental control.

"If you don't want to do this with me, tell me now. I won't put this baby through what my father did to me." I don't even dare look at Adrian as I say those words to him. I can't bear to see his face if he doesn't want to be in our lives.

The car pulls over so fast it makes my head dizzy.

Adrian is out of the driver side and opening my door in a blink of an eye. Kneeling down so that he's level with me, he spins me in the seat, not pulling me from the car, but enough that I'm facing him.

"I have never wanted anything more in my life. I want you and this baby."

I look into his hazel eyes; they are glistening with unshed tears.

"I just." Not finishing, not knowing what I'm even trying to say. I look away, trying to understand my own emotions.

He grabs my face, cupping it with both his hands, holding me.

"No, Angel, listen to me. I know I fucked up, and I know I don't deserve you, but I can't and won't live my life without you. Baby or no baby, you were always going to be mine."

His words should scare me, but they don't. It's everything I wanted to hear.

Tears stream down my face as I become a blubbering mess.

"Adrian, I love you; I want to be yours," I manage to blab out.

"No doubt of that, Angel." He then kisses me, showing me in that kiss exactly how he feels. He didn't have to say the words for me to know.

When he pulls away, tucks my feet back into the car, and closes the door to walk back around, I can't help but laugh and smile. Nothing we have done since the night we met has been normal or conventional, but it all feels so right at this moment.

Getting back in the driver seat, he puts the car in drive and pulls off the shoulder.

"Let's go show your little brother a good birthday." He smiles over at me.

Adrian

I don't think I have ever felt the kind of joy I felt seeing that little blob on the monitor, seeing my baby, our baby. I didn't think anything could make me happier than that moment.

That was until Emmy told me she loved me.

I should have said it back, but the first time those words are said to her, it won't be on the side of the road.

It doesn't take long for us to reach the park.

I can't believe what I see when we get there. Balloons and streamers are covering a pavilion next to the play set, and the tables are covered in bright-color tablecloths.

There's a decent-size sheet cake on the table and some wrapped gifts.

Holding Emmy's hand, we walk toward Ryan and Joanne. The boys are playing in the jungle gym.

"What's all this?" I ask Ryan as we approach.

"Couldn't very well leave the kid without a proper birthday," he says, smiling.

"Wow, this is amazing," Emmy says.

Joanne turns from watching the boys play and joins us.

"How did the appointment go?"

I squeeze Emmy's hand.

"Well, we are definitely pregnant," she says and offers her mom one of the little sonogram pictures.

Joanne takes the picture smiling. "Oh, my gosh, look at that," she says. Then hands the little picture to Ryan, he takes it, looking it over, then looks back at me.

"Congrats, brother," he says, trying to hide the emotion in his voice.

"Thank you." Letting go of Emmy's hand, I pull my brother into a hug and pat him on the back.

I know I have a long way back to get into his good graces again, but he's my brother, my family, and I know no matter what, he's going to be there for me through this.

He clears his throat and steps back. Emmy smiles and takes the sonogram from Ryan.

It's a weird situation, but we will make it work.

"How have the boys been?" she asks.

"Great, Dillon is a smart kid; he was a bit standoffish for a while, but he's come around. And Davis is just a little ball of energy, so happy," Joanne answers.

"Heard any more about their dad?" Ryan asks me.

Shaking my head, I answer, "Not yet; he seems to have just disappeared. I wish I knew where to even look."

"I don't know; I don't think he has any family left in the area," Joanne offers.

"Emmwy, you came!" an excited little Davis yells, running up to Emmy and jumping for her.

I wince as she tries to catch him but gets knocked over, falling to the ground with the little boy. I immediately went to grab her, afraid she got hurt.

Helping her up, she and Davis are both laughing.

"You okay, Angel?" I ask, worried.

"I'm fine."

"Sawy, Emmwy," Davis says, noticing my sharp tone.

"I'm okay, Davis," she reassures him.

Davis looks up at me.

"I didn't mean to scare you, little buddy; we just have to be gentle with Emmy, okay?"

"Okay, Mister Man."

"Are you ready for some cake and ice cream?" Joanne asked.

"Yup, yup," Davis says, and luckily returns to his energetic self when he looks over at the cake and presents.

"I'll go get Dillon," Emmy says, looking around the playground.

I help Davis climb up to the table, setting him directly in front of the cake. Ryan gets out a knife and spatula while Joanne grabs plates and the ice cream from a cooler I hadn't noticed tucked under the table earlier.

They really went all out to make this day special, and for a kid they did know before this morning, and one who happens to be the son of Joannes ex. It was a little mind-blowing seeing Ryan like this; he'd be a really good dad.

Buzzzzz

My phone vibrating in my pocket pulls my attention away from my thoughts.

Pulling the phone out, Anthony's name flashes on the screen. I hit answer and walk away from the pavilion, taking stock of where Emmy is before walking too far away.

"Anything new?" I ask.
"Boss, they found him."

I sigh in relief. At least that's one thing. The next part will be to try and get him help and keep these boys out of his hands.

"Good, he's missing his son's birthday," I say.
"Ugh, boss."
"What is it, Anthony?"
"It's not good, not good at all."

Why can't things just go smoothly? Running my hand through my hair, I seek out Emmy; she's still over by the play set talking to Dillon; they look to be in a conversation.
She looks up and smiles at me. I give her a small nod.

"What happened?"
"Bruno found him; he was on the property; guess he just never made it in." There's a brief pause. *"Boss, he, ugh, he's in bad shape, barely alive. Bruno said he isn't sure he's going to make it."*
"Fuck!"

How the hell was I going to tell his kids—all of them? That their dad is likely going to die; it's not that I give a shit about that fuckin prick, but I care about who he's hurting.

"Bruno had to call it in; the police will likely be reaching out to Emmy."
"Thanks for the heads up."
"If you need anything, let me know."
"Thanks, man."

I end the call and walk back toward the small party.

Emmy and Dillon walk over hand in hand at the same time. Standing next to each other, you can see the similarities between them—the shape of their eyes and nose, their eye color. It's crazy. It makes me wonder if our little one will have those same honey eyes.

Patting his shoulder, she says something to him, and he runs off to grab some cake.

"Everything all right?" Emmy asks, coming to my side.

I can't tell her here, now.

"It was Anthony with an update."

"They found him?"

I nod.

"Not here, Angel; we'll talk when this is over."

She gives me a knowing look, something crosses her features, but she quickly puts a smile back on. I kiss the top of her head.

Wishing I could take away all shit she's going through, wishing I didn't have to tell her about James. It would have almost been better if he wasn't found at all.

Wrapping an arm around her, I tuck her into my side, and we join the others for cake and ice cream.

Emmy

I noticed after Davis had run over from the playground that Dillon had stayed back, where he was currently sitting alone on a hanging bridge.

"I'll go get Dillon," I offer, walking to join him on the bridge that is suspended only a foot off the ground between the two main parts of the equipment.

"Can I join you?" I ask him.

"Sure." He kicks the sand below his feet.

"I know things are a little crazy, but I hope you know we are just looking out for you."

Dillon may be a kid, but he's smart, and I have no doubt that he's seen and understands exactly what's going on. I could tell when we picked them up from the car that he had to be Davis's protector.

"You're my sister, right?" he asks, looking up at me.

"How did you know that?"

"Dad and Mom used to fight about you."

"I'm sorry your parents fought about me."

He shrugs. "They fought about everything."

"I'm sorry I didn't know about you; I would have tried to be in your life."

"You want to be my sister?" he asks nervously.

"Of course, I do," I say.

He grins up at me genuinely for the first time. "I'm glad you found us."

"Me too."

Sensing Adrian, I look up and notice he's on the phone. He looks over at me. He looks stressed, and I can only guess who he's talking with.

Turning my attention back to Dillon. "You want to go get some cake?"

"Yes, please."

Standing, I hold my hand out to him. He jumps up from the bridge and takes my hand.

"Your mom is really nice," he says as we walk.

"She is, *huh*?"

"Yeah, we even got to play with the dogs earlier. I always wanted a dog."

"I'm sure she will let you play with them whenever you want."

He looks at me and crunches his lips together, clearly thinking about it.

When we reach the pavilion, Adrian is also walking back. I pat Dillon on the shoulder.

"Go get some cake."

He runs off.

Walking up to Adrian, I can tell something isn't right.

"Everything all right?" I ask.

He straightens, holding back something.

"It was Anthony with an update."

"They found him?"

He just nods to me.

"Not here, Angel; we'll talk when this is over."

I know that it can't be good. He's locked up or worse, and from his demeanor, I have a feeling it's the latter.

A strange mix of emotions comes over me, but I quickly shake it off, forcing a smile.

He kisses the top of my head.

Wrapping an arm around my waist, he pulls me into his side, and we join the others for cake and ice cream.

James has taken a lot from all of us, and I won't let him take any more from these boys. Davis is going to get the best birthday, and we will deal with whatever else tomorrow.

* * *

After cake, ice cream, presents, and a lot of laughing with the kids, Davis has so much energy; he's like a walking red bull ad. I'm just happy that the absence of James didn't distract him from his day, and he was still able to have fun. He had asked where he was once, but my mom had done a good job diverting his attention.

Now that little ball of energy was convincing my mom and Ryan that their house was the best place to have a sleepover.

I guess my small apartment was no match compared to a house with dogs.

We gather up the party stuff and are loading it into the back of Ryan's Cresting SUV when I notice two cop cars pulling into the parking lot.

I immediately look around for Adrian; he's helping pull down streamers. Then I scan the area for the boys, who are luckily distracted, playing on the playground.

It could be a coincidence; they might not be here for us at all. After all, how would they know the boys were here?

Putting the last bag in, I close the hatch.

The officers are making their way toward me. I walk closer to them, glancing over my shoulder, my mom is over by the boys, and Ryan and Adrian are still doing clean-up none of them have noticed yet. I don't want the boys to see them.

My heart pounds in my chest as I meet the officers a few feet away from the car.

"Miss Johnson?" one of the officers asks.

"Yes."

I notice one of the other officers looking over at my brothers.

"What can I do for you?" I ask nervously.

"When was the last time you talked to James Johnson?"

"Yesterday afternoon."

"And where were you last night around ten p.m.?"

"What is this about?" I ask, wondering why they are asking these types of questions. What has James really done I wonder.

The officer, who has been quiet this whole time, steps closer. "James was found earlier today, he's in the hospital on life support."

I start to shake; I don't even know what I should be feeling.

"I'm sorry, what?" I ask, making sure I heard him right.

"James has been found near death, likely not going to make it through the day, and we are trying to retrace his last steps."

"And you think I had something to do with it?"

"That's not what we are saying, ma'am; we are just piecing some things together."

I look over at the boys who are walking this direction, hand in hand with my mom. I want to stop them; I don't want them to see the officers.

"Can we do this somewhere else?" I ask shakily.

The officers look toward the boys and back to me.

"They will need to come with us."

"What? No!" I screech.

Adrian runs over to me.

"What's going on here?" He places a hand on my shoulder and looks at the officers.

"They want to take Dillon and Davis," I say, in a sob.

"That's not going to happen, Angel," he says to me, looking down into my eyes, but his tone lets me know; it's meant for them too.

"Excuse me, but who are you?" the first officer asks.

"Adrian Montgomery."

"Oh good, we needed to talk to you as well."

"We can do that somewhere other than here, and it will not involve the boys," Adrian tells the officer.

"That isn't up to you, Mr. Montgomery; with their father being unresponsive, they will be taken into state custody now."

"But I'm their sister."

My heart breaks even further as Dillon runs up to me. He must have heard the officers.

He grabs the back of my leg; for the first time, he seems so small.

"Emmy dad not coming back?"

Sinking to the ground, I turn and wrap Dillon in my arms. Adrian crosses his arms over his chest and steps in front of us, blocking the cops from us.

"No, buddy, I don't think he's coming back this time." I have never seen him be anything other than serious, but now he's vulnerable, and there are tears in his eyes. I look over his back and see that my mom has Davis in her arms; he's clinging to her, his head tucked into her neck. She's standing back by the pavilion, and I'm thankful she is.

"It's going to be okay, buddy, I won't leave you alone."

I stand holding him to my side, Adrian steps back to us, wrapping his arm around my shoulder.

"We still have some questions for you, Mr. Montgomery, as well as you, Miss Johnson."

"That's fine, we will answer whatever you need, but the boys will be going home with my mom," I say.

"She isn't next of kin," the officer argues.

It's at that moment that Ryan walks over; he has his phone to his ear.

"Officers, I'm Ryan Montgomery, and Joanne and I will be taking custody of Dillon and Davis effective immediately, and we have filed a petition with the court for full guardianship under the current circumstances. I have my lawyer on the phone if you'd like to talk to him," he offers his phone to the officer.

At the same time, a voice comes over the officer's radio, telling him to call in. He looks back at the quiet cop, who walks to the patrol car. I can see him on the phone and looking a little pail as he comes back to us.

"That won't be necessary, Mr. Montgomery," the quiet officer says. "You and Mrs. Montgomery are free to go with the boys."

Ryan nods in a gesture of agreement. "Thank you."

He reaches a hand to Dillon, who is still gripping my leg tightly. Dillon looks up at me, then to Ryan. I give him a soft smile.

"It's okay, go with them. I will see you later I promise."

Reluctantly, he lets me go and takes Ryan's hand.

My mom and Davis join them, and I watch as they load in the SUV.

"You, however, need to come down to the station and answer some more questions." The officer gestures to myself and Adrian.

We agreed to meet them there. One car pulls in front of us, and the other follows us back to the station.

When we were in the car, I let out a stream of emotion.

"I don't understand why they need to talk to us."

"I'm sure it's just standard, Angel. They have nothing to keep us on, or we wouldn't be driving our own car to the station."

"But they are making it seem like I did something wrong, that I'm the reason he's in the hospital." I can't help the dread and uneasy feeling.

How could they not tell it was an accident or an overdose?

"Do you think those biker guys he pissed off did something to him? I have to ask; I don't know them."

Adrian looks over at me.

"I don't think they would waste their time with him. What reason would they have to go that far? He wasn't anyone to them."

"I don't know; I'm just trying to figure it out." I shake my head.

I was tense by the time we finally pull into the police station.

Wishing my best friend was here for all this. I could really use Lucy right now.

Adrian helps me out of the car, lacing his fingers with mine as we walk in.

Adrian

After two long hours of answering questions and providing bar footage, Emmy and I were finally released to go.

She has been so strong through all this, answering everything they have thrown at her.

I didn't like James one bit, and I had only met him that brief moment in the bar. Regardless of how I feel about him or the fact that he was not in her life much, he's her father, and I know this can't be easy on her.

All I want is to get her home; she looks exhausted and like she's ready to completely break down.

Emmy insisted we stop by Ryan and Joannes first though, which I can't fault her for. I wanted to check on them as well.

I'm still reeling with shock at what Ryan had told the officers—were they really planning to take full custody of the boys? When had they even decided that? And how did he get that handled so quickly? I can only guess at the amount of money he had to have thrown around to make that happen.

Walking into the front room, Davis is on the floor, rolling around with Zeek, laughing. Dillon is sitting on the couch watching a cartoon with talking dogs on the TV.

As they see us walk in, Davis jumps up from the floor and runs toward us.

"Emmwy!" He squeals.

I brace behind her, waiting for the impact of the little ball of energy, but he skids to a stop right before he reaches her, then slowly wraps his arms around her.

She lets out a small laugh.

"I being gentle, Emmwy."

"Good job, little man," I say and ruffle his hair.

I'm rewarded with a big toothy grin. He lets go of Emmy as Zeek and Tank flank him, wagging their tails.

He reaches out simultaneously, petting both of them. And in a matter of minutes, he's back to wrestling them and is as happy as can be.

Ryan and Joanne are watching from the kitchen island. Emmy walks over to them, but I walk over to Dillon, who hasn't done more than glance over at us when we first got here.

"Can I sit?" I ask him.

"Sure."

"What ya watching?"

"Paw Patrol," he answers.

"Aww, I haven't seen that one. I'm more a Teenage Mutant Ninja Turtles guy," I say.

"Ninja Turtles?"

"You haven't seen the Ninja Turtles?" I ask in mock horror.

"No, he shakes his head."

"They are the coolest; there are four of them: Leonardo, Donatello, Michelangelo, and Raphael; they live in the sewer, but it's not gross, and they train with a rat that is like their dad; his name is Master Splinter, and they fight off bad guys like The Shredder."

"They sound weird, turtles that are ninja's."

"No weirder than dogs in clothes making rescues." I shrug.

"*Hmm,* true, maybe I'll have to watch the turtle thing sometime."

"Oh definitely, Ryan probably still has the action figures," I add.

His eyes light up at that.

"You doing okay?" I ask him now that I've got him loosened up a bit.

He slouches his shoulders a little. "We were left alone a lot... But I miss him."

"Of course, you do, buddy; you probably always will. And it's okay to be confused, hurt, sad, and all the other things you're probably feeling. Do you want to try and go see him in the hospital?"

"Is he going to come out of the hospital?" he asks.

"Not looking like it; he's not awake, but if you want to see him, we can take you." I don't know if this is the right way to handle this type of situation, but Dillon is a smart kid, and I don't want to lie to him.

"No, I don't want to; I saw my mom like that, and I don't want to do that again."

My heart breaks for all these boys have been through in their short lives.

He straightens and looks at me seriously.

"Does Emmy not want to be my sister now?"

"What? Of course, she still wants to be your sister."

"But Ryan and Joanne asked if we would like to live here with them; they even got us bunk beds to sleep in."

"Oh, buddy, that doesn't mean that Emmy doesn't want you; Joanne is Emmy's mom, like Tina was your mom. Joanne just wants to take care of you like she took care of Emmy."

I don't know how to explain this kind of thing to a seven-year-old, and I hope I'm not saying anything wrong.

He looks over the back of the couch and smiles as he looks at Emmy and Joanne, who are talking in the kitchen.

"You understand what I'm saying?"

"Yes."

"If you don't want to live here, we can figure something else out, but we will always be in your life, Emmy isn't going anywhere, okay?"

"I like it here, and Davis RE-EALLY likes it here."

He drags out and emphasizes really while shaking his head and looking down at his little brother, who is in a pile of fur just lying on the dogs on the floor, half asleep. All three crazy animals are apparently tired out.

"I'm glad; Ryan is the best guy I know; he will make sure you have absolutely everything you could ever need."

I pat him on the knee, then get up from the couch, and he turns his attention back to the TV.

"So, you want to take this all on?" I ask Ryan as I join them in the kitchen.

"I couldn't think of anything else I could want more than to provide a stable, loving environment for those boys; they deserve better than they have been dealt so far."

Emmy's eyes tear up at Ryan's words.

"I can take them," she says.

"You have so much on your plate, baby girl; you are about to start a whole new chapter in your life, and as much as I know you could handle all of it, this is mine and Ryan's chance to do something to make it easier on you and easier on them. They are going to need lots of guidance and strong parental help. Be their sister; they are going to need that too."

I wrap my arm around Emmy and pull her flush against me, her back to my front, and kiss the top of her head. My hand splayed palm across her lower abdomen.

"They are okay with the idea, Angel. And your mom is right. They are going to need to have you to come to as they get older, especially when they disagree with their parental figure." I half chuckle at the end.

"Okay," she says reluctantly.

Placing her hand on top of mine over her stomach. I can see the idea of leaving them is hard for her.

"Can I take you home yet?"

"Please, I feel dead on my feet."

We say our goodbyes. Emmy checks in with the boys, triple-checking that they are okay here and promising to see them tomorrow.

We haven't told Davis about James yet; he doesn't need that on his birthday. He knows something crazy bad happened at the end of his party but not what. Then he was too excited about playing with the dogs to care about anything else. I envy the resilience of kids.

* * *

Just as predicted, James didn't make it through the night. Which left so many more questions unanswered. The police finally let us know why they had been so adamant about questioning Emmy. When they had searched James' belongings, they uncovered info on his phone that he had been planning to try and blackmail Emmy for money. He was going to use her brothers as leverage in hopes to get her to pay him; he had assumed after seeing her in the grocery store that she had money to give.

Because of that, the police had wanted to make certain his overdose hadn't been the result of foul play, retaliation if she had found out about the blackmail.

It's been two weeks since the whole ordeal—two weeks that the boys have been settling in with Ryan and Joanne. The first week was crazy. Emmy and Joanne took care of everything to give the boys a proper funeral for their father.

Ryan had pulled a lot of strings to get custody of those boys, but I have to commend him for it; he truly cares about them.

He even insisted they see a counselor, and I couldn't have agreed more. Better they find ways to deal with everything now than have it eat at them later. Overall, they have done very well adjusting to all the new things in their lives. I haven't left Emmy's side since it all happened; all of this has taken a toll on her. This past week, she has been in a funk, dealing with the loss herself.

I know as much as anyone that the words I say to her do very little to help her get through it; it's something she has to work through herself. I can only show her I'm still here, and if she wants to talk it out with me, I'll listen.

With everything going on, it also means we haven't talked about us and what she wants. If it's up to me, it won't be long until I'm changing her last name.

It doesn't matter to me how quickly things happened for us, she is my future.

Emmy

I have struggled with losing James worse than I could have imagined; my emotions have been all over the place, and I have been dealing with some highs and lows.

It's hard to explain to someone what grief feels like when you lose the man who was supposed to be there for you—the man you used to wish would come back in your life one day. The reason you did everything to be the best growing up, the thoughts of a delusional little girl who thought that somehow, if she were good enough then her dad would want to be with her and no one else would leave.

All that was wrong, though; he never wanted me, and the second he came back into my life, all he wanted was to abandon his other kids and try to get money from me.

What kind of person does that?

The first week after he overdosed, there was a whirlwind of police and DCFs, and planning a funeral so that Davis and Dillon could say goodbye.

It was after that when things started to calm that it got worse for me.

It gave me too much time to think, and I couldn't help feeling like I was failing the boys, just like he had me, how I wasn't going to be good enough.

When Ryan and my mom said they were going to take the boys, I struggled with it, even though I never told anyone. I felt like letting that happen was me taking the easy way out by letting them raise them instead of me, and they weren't family I was, I was their older sister; they were counting on me.

If I couldn't be there for them, then how was I going to be a good mom? There were a few days I let the dark thoughts take over, and I didn't get out of bed at all.

It took me time to realize that none of that was true.

Being with them was truly what was best for Dillon and Davis that was the most stable environment for them.

Adrian has been here nonstop since it happened. I have been emotionally unavailable to him, yet he still stayed. He has shown me he is here.

He made sure I ate something and sat with me, not forcing me to talk about how I was feeling. He didn't put pressure on me to snap out of it. He was just there.

It helped me recognize that we will be far better parents than James could have ever been. That realization was part of what brought me out of the funk. If I was going to be a better parent, I needed to take care of myself so that I could take care of this baby.

Finally feeling a little better and less in a funk I shower and get ready for the first time in days.

I am greeted with the smell of bacon when I enter the kitchen. Adrian turns from the stove and smiles at me. My heart stutters.

"Good morning, beautiful, hungry?"

"Starving."

"Good, have a seat."

Adrian places a plate of eggs, bacon, and a cup of tea in front of me as I take a seat on the bar stool.

"This looks amazing; thank you."

I say around a big bite of bacon. Shutting off the stove and grabbing another plate, Adrian comes around and joins me.

This is the first day I have eaten next to him since we buried James.

"I'm sorry."

"Angel, nothing to be sorry about."

"I kind of spiraled for a bit."

Adrian grabs my face gently, turning my chin to look at him. I look in his hazel eyes. He leans down and kisses me softly.

"It's okay, Angel. I spiraled for years. I think you're still ahead of the game here."

I can't help but laugh, and I swat him away.

He backs up and smiles at me. His hazel eyes danced with mischief. I don't know how he always knows what I need, but, gawds, I love him for it.

He stands, reaching for my plate to clean up. I stop him, grabbing his wrist.

"Leave it."

He drops the plate.

"Anything you say."

I slide off the stool, walking back to the bedroom. Adrian follows.

He has been so patient with me, and I want to reward him.

When we reach the room, I strip down while Adrian watches me from the doorway. Once all layers of clothing have come off, I turn to face him.

"So fucking beautiful," he says, stepping fully into the room. He closes the bedroom door, even though there is no one else here.

He picks me up, kissing me, and I wrap my legs around his waist.

The familiar spark between us sends my body into a frenzy.

I pull back from the kiss, still hanging on him.

"This reminds me of our first time—me vulnerable and you with far too many clothes on."

He sets me on my feet. Quickly stripping himself until there is nothing between us.

"I think I need to be punished for letting you go so long without any," I say.

"*Hmm.*" His eyes scan over my body. "What did you have in mind, Angel?"

I walk over to the bedside table, pulling a coiled bundle of soft rope out. Walking back to Adrian, I hand him the pink rope. His eyes light up.

"You sure?"

I nod.

"I'm going to need you to answer that one out loud."

"Yes, I'm sure."

"Kneel down on the bed, facing away from me, hands behind your back."

I do as he says, and my body tingles with excitement.

"Pick a safe word, Angel."

I'm comfortable with him; after the first night together, I know he won't push me.

"I don't need one; I trust you."

"No, Angel, you always need one; it doesn't matter how much you trust me, how much control you are giving me; you need a safe word; you always have a choice when this stops or is too much."

"*Um*, Chips."

Adrian chuckles. "Chips?"

"Yes chips. Cuz it's probably because I want a bag of chips."

"*Ah*, I see, cravings already."

"The only thing I am craving right now is you. Don't keep me waiting."

Adrian comes up to the bed, rubbing the rope from the nape of my neck down my spine. It leaves a trail of goosebumps. Leaning down, he blows a soft breath on the back of my neck, and it takes all my control to not move.

"Wouldn't dream of keeping you waiting, baby."

Taking the rope, Adrian starts at my wrists, which he has pulled together behind my back, straightening my arms out. He begins by halving the rope, taking the center loop around my wrist, pulling the ends back through the loop on the other side, he gently works his way up my arms, twisting the rope around my arms and knotting in the center. Once he's to my shoulder blades, he takes the rope, over my shoulders criss crossing over and under my breasts, he wraps around my back and to the front again sliding the rope around itself in front and knotting the ends. By the time he's finished, my breathing is deeper; my nipples have peaked. He's created a beautiful bondage around my chest and arms. I am fully at his mercy.

"You look stunning."

From behind, he trails kisses from my hands up my arms, stopping at the nape of my neck. He kisses the soft spot just below my ear that drives me crazy.

"So fucking perfect," he praises.

"Off your knees, Angel. Flip around and sit on the edge of the bed."

I carefully move so that I am on my ass; it's a miracle I didn't fall on my face, flipping my legs out from under me.

Adrian is standing in front of me, his hand on his cock.

He takes in my nipples one at a time, sucking them between his teeth and nipping at them. I want to grab him and run my fingers through his hair. But I can't; I can't move. It's both exhilarating and torture.

"You know I really should punish you for selling that painting of yourself."

"I, *ugh,* it wasn't."

He cuts me off. "Now, Angel, don't pretend that wasn't you; you and I both know it was. And you know what?"

"What?" I ask.

"No one gets what's mine, and you are mine."

"I'm sorry, I wasn't thinking."

"No, you weren't, but you will make it up to me, won't you, Angel?"

"Yes."

He kisses me, splitting my lips with his tongue and devouring me with his.

He pinches my nipples, and I moan. Pulling back, he stands tall, he grabs the rope that's crossed just above my breasts, and pulls me to my feet.

"Turn around and spread your legs."

I do as he says without hesitation. One hand on my waist, the other sliding down my hip, to the front of my body, he stops at the junction of my legs, kissing my shoulder blade. He steps closer so that he's now pressed against me, his hard cock touching my bound hands. He slips his hand down further, finding my clit. I shiver into him, and as he flicks and rubs, wrapping around my body, he slips a finger into me.

"So fucking ready for me."

I'm panting and breathless, so close to climax. And then he stops. Pulling his hand away and stepping back.

"I. What." I stumble over my words in shock.

"I told you, you were going to be punished."

Stepping back up to me, he whispers in my ear.

"Luckily for you, I found the painting and bought it back."

"You what?" I ask.

"*Shhh...* Angel. Be a good girl and bend over that bed for me."

Flabbergasted I do it. I bend over, spreading my legs wider, and tilting my head so that my cheek lays on the mattress.

"That's it, baby; you look so fucking perfect, tied up, pussy glistening for me."

Adrian

Gripping my cock, I step between her legs. I rub the tip along her slip, she moans, and it's the sexiest fucking sound. She's fucking perfection. How I got so lucky, I will never know.

Without warning, I slam into her, gripping her hips and pulling her back into me. The sounds that escape her are like music as I pump in and out of her, careful to keep from pressing her too hard into the bed. I can feel her getting close again, and this time I won't deny her her release.

"That's it, Angel."

"Harder, I won't break," she says through panting breaths.

Who am I to say what she can handle?

I grab the rope midway up her tied arms and hold onto it tightly as I fuck her harder.

She clenches down, shaking as she rides the wave of ecstasy. I follow her with my own release.

Laying her back down to the bed, I slowly pull out of her. My cum drips down her leg, and I don't think I have ever seen a better sight. All my primal desires rise. I would put a baby in her if she wasn't already pregnant. This woman is my everything.

"I love you, Emmy," I say as I reach under her and begin to unwrap her bondage.

She takes an audible breath.

"You okay?" I ask in concern.

"Perfect."

Pausing, I pull her to her feet, turning her so I can look her in the eyes. She has fresh tears on her cheeks. I reach up one hand and rub my thumb across her cheek, wiping the tear.

"Did I hurt you?"

"No, no. Hurry and un wrap me, though, please." I make quick work of the rest of the rope dropping it to the floor.

Before I can ask again, her wobbly arms come around my neck, and she pulls me down into her kissing me hard and fast. Taken off guard, we sway, and I have to spin us so she lands on top of me as we topple to the ground.

She laughs as she lands on me, our naked bodies a tangle of limbs.

I blink up at her. Has she gone mad?

"I love you too," she finally says through her giggles.

Sitting up and holding her to me. I kiss her forehead.

"That was the first time you've said it to me," she adds.

I hadn't realized it was; I don't even know when I knew I loved her. I had known she was special to me the first day in the bar. How had I not told her yet? I know the past couple weeks have been a little crazy, with the funeral, making sure the boys were settling in, and her dealing with her depression, but I can't believe I hadn't said it before now.

"I would spend another twelve years suffering if it meant I had you at the end. Since the day I met you, I knew that you were mine… My world was empty and lonely. You filled it up, Angel. I love you more than I have ever loved anyone before. More than I knew, one could love someone."

More tears spilling from her eyes.

"I don't know how we got here, Adrian, but here with you is the only place I want to be."

Emmy
Months Later

Taking a minute to get off my feet being largely pregnant, my position on this couch and in this dress is not the most flattering, but its comfortable. I pull out my phone and open the notepad. Laughing at the silly note I started months ago to remind myself of the mistakes I made trying to have a one-night stand.

Sometimes, it feels like a lifetime ago, and sometimes it still feels like yesterday. I would make those same mistakes all over again. It doesn't matter to me what anyone else might think about our relationship.

The dynamics of our family may be a little weird, with Grandpa technically being uncle too when this little one is born, but that doesn't matter, nor does it need to be explained. What matters is that this baby is so loved already, with a Dad who is overjoyed and Dillon and Davis who can't wait to be uncles and help with the baby.

I smile looking at the note, making a few changes. Changes I am happy to live with.

How <u>NOT</u> to have a one-night stand
~~Never~~ go home with a stranger from the bar
~~Never~~ develop feelings for the guy

~~Never~~ invite him to stay over a second night
~~Never ever~~, have sex with him a second time
~~Never~~ get knocked up…
Fall in love
Marry the man

Marrying Adrian in December was the best Christmas present I had ever received.

"Why are you hiding in here, Angel?"

"Needed to get off my feet for a minute."

My heart rate picks up as he walks over, and the way he's looking at me, it's the same way he did that first night, with all the need and desire in his beautiful hazel eyes.

He's even wearing a black button-up shirt with the sleeves rolled just above his elbows.

Leaning down, one hand pressed on the arm of the sofa at my side, the other on my stomach.

He leans down and kisses me softly.

"Do you even know what seeing you walking around in this dress has been doing to me all night?"

The dress is a light green A-Line Pleated Stretch Satin floor-length with a slit up the side. The way I'm sitting has it covering most of me, with just one knee poking out of the slit.

I shiver as he slides his hand from my belly to the exposed knee, causing the satin fabric to slide down, exposing more of me.

His touch caused a moan to slip past my lips.

"Do you want to close that door?" I ask him, hoping the answer is yes.

He chuckles. "There is a room full of people wanting your attention, Angel. If I close that door, everyone in that room will know what I am doing to you in here."

I huff and push him back.

"Fine, help me up then."

He grabs my hand, and I uncross my legs as he helps pull me to my feet. As he does, my phone clammers to the ground, forgotten when he entered the room.

Adrian picks it up, looking at the screen.

"What is this?" he asks, raising an eyebrow at me.

I feel the heat rush my cheeks.

"A silly note. I started a while ago."

I watch as he reads over the list. A smile crosses his face.

"I like the amendments. I would just add a couple more things."

He taps on the screen, then hands it back to me.

How <u>NOT</u> to have a one-night stand
~~Never~~ go home with a stranger from the bar
~~Never~~ develop feelings for the guy
~~Never~~ invite him to stay over a second night
~~Never ever~~, have sex with him ~~a second time~~ A LOT
~~Never~~ get knocked up...
Fall in love
Marry the man
Live Happily Ever After

That is exactly what I intend to do.

Epilogue
Adrian

"You're going to have to be quieter than that angel. Your mom is downstairs with Evelyn and Ryan, and the boys will be here any minute."

"My mom is here?" she whispers, between breaths.

"Yes, Angel. I saw her walk in on the monitor."

She turns her head to look over her shoulder. Looking at the monitors on the other side of the room that show the multiple security camera angles from around the house, Joanne has Evelyn, our two-year-old in the kitchen, putting her in her high chair.

"Now be a good girl and stay quiet," I say before continuing to lap at her sweet pussy.

She presses her lips tightly together, inhaling deeply through her nose, pulling at the velvety cuff restraints at her wrists.

Her body begins to shake as I pump two fingers into her, curving them upward to hit that spot I know she loves, while licking and sucking on her clit.

"That's it, baby; give me what I want."

Her release comes in waves, the walls of her pussy clenching around my fingers as I slow my pumping, letting her ride out her orgasm.

When her body stops convulsing and her breathing slows, I remove my fingers, smiling down at her, her beautiful honey eyes open, watching me as I lick them clean.

"You know how much I love the taste of you," I say, my tongue smacking my lips as I suck up every drop.

"Your turn," she says.

And as much as I want to bury myself deep inside her. We have a house full downstairs now.

I lean across her, uncuff her wrist.

"We will have to finish later, love; we have guests."

I climb off the bed and head to the attached bathroom to clean up.

I'm only in there a minute when Emmy walks in, and I turn around to face her. She's pulled on a pale-yellow sundress that makes her hair seem even brighter, making her look ever like the angel she is to me.

"I can't let you go out with that," she says, pointing to my still-hard cock, that's already dripping with pre-cum.

Before I can argue, she drops to her knees on the plush rug, grabbing hold of my erection and taking it into her mouth. She sucks in, hollowing out her cheeks around me, bobbing up and down. I rock my hips forward as she sucks, fucking her pretty little mouth. It's not long before I explode, cum coating her throat, and like the good girl she is, she swallows it all.

Emmy

Standing, I kiss Adrian on the cheek, reach for the mouthwash and rinse before walking out of the bathroom. Pausing before our bed, I look up at the painting that hangs over the headboard. A painting I never thought I would see again. It's the painting of a curious, naive girl wrapped in rope. Adrian has never told me how it became in his possession, but when I look at it now, I no longer see the innocence in it; I see it as a start to the woman I was becoming, the one who now gets to experience great things both sexually and emotionally with the most amazing stranger from a bar.

With the biggest smile on my face, I head down to join our guests in the kitchen.

Stopping at the highchair, kissing the top of Evelyn's head, her dirty blonde hair a mess of curls, she coos and giggles, smiling up at me with the same hazel eyes as her daddy. The greens, blues, and browns swirl amongst each other in the best kaleidoscope of color. Momma, Momma," she says.

"Hey, baby girl, have you been good for Grandma?"

Her little head bobs up and down, curls bouncing about.

"She was great," my mom says walking to stand by me.

"You came back a little earlier than expected," I tell her.

"Someone had to get this place ready; we both know you were too busy to do it." She chastises me. But smiles.

Looking around, I notice she has already decorated the place.

"Ryan is out on that amazing patio of yours, firing up the grill in that outdoor kitchen already," she adds.

Adrian comes down the stairs then. "Don't let him touch my grill." He walks past the kitchen, pausing briefly to kiss Evelyn and myself on the cheek.

"Dillon, come help me show your dad how a real grill master does it," he calls toward the front room, where Dillon and Davis were both playing on the game console.

Dillon jumps up from the couch and runs toward the patio. "*Ugh*, he's going to get me killed, leaving the game in the middle of the match," Davis says.

I laugh. Davis has not slowed down in the past two years; he's still ever the hyper-go-go kid and takes his video games very seriously. Where Dillon enjoys doing things with the adults and plays games only when he's bored.

"When will Lucy be here?" my mom asks.

I look at the clock.

"Any time now, I'm sure. I told her the party starts at one, and it's a quarter to."

"Did you see Evelyn's cake?" I ask.

"Yes, so cute, unicorns; she's going to love it," my mom says.

It's not long before the guests are all here. We have a house full of our closest friends and family, all celebrating my little girl's second birthday. I stand to the side as she finishes ripping open her gifts with Davis's help.

I know Adrian is walking up beside me without even looking. That tingle that spreads through me every time he's near gives him away.

"I think this has been a very successful day, Angel."

"It has indeed," I say tiptoeing so that I can kiss his cheek.

He grabs around my waist. Making me squeal as he spins me so that my back is to his front.

His warm breath on my ear as he whispers, "I think later we should try and make her a sibling."

I lean back into him.

"You think so?" I smile, tilting my head back.

Both eyes dart forward when my mom squeals. But I'm not surprised.

I can feel Adrian straighten behind me as he finally sees why my mom squealed.

"For real?" my mom says and holds up Evelyn's last present.

"For real," I answer, reading the adorable shirt I had made for her, well, and for Adrian.

Promoted to Big Sister

Written across it.

"Well, that isn't going to stop me from still trying," Adrian jokes. I elbow him in the rib.

He winces, faking like it hurts.

"Have I told you lately how happy you make me, Angel?"

"It was a condition you added," I remind him. He wraps his arms around me tighter. Kissing the top of my head.

"And they lived happily ever after."

The End